Jesus at Walmart

...the Cost

rickleland.com

Jesus at Walmart...the Cost

Published by:
Freedom Shores Media
South Haven, MI

Scripture references are from the HOLY BIBLE, as follows:

KING JAMES VERSION.

THE NEW KING JAMES, Copyright©1982 by Thomas Nelson, Inc. Used by permission.

NEW INTERNATIONAL VERSION. Copyright © 1984 by the International Bible Society. Used by permission of Zondervan Publishing. All rights reserved.

THE MESSAGE © 1993. Used by permission of NavPress Publishing Group.

GOOD NEWS TRANSLATION©1976 by the American Bible Society. Used by permission. All rights reserved.

NEW AMERICAN STANDARD BIBLE © Copyright 1960, 1962, 1963, 1971, 1973, 1975, 1977, 1995 by the Lockman Foundation. Used by permission.

NEW LIVING TRANSLATION, copyright © 1996, 2004, 2007 by Tyndale House Foundation. Used by permission of Tyndale House Publishers, Inc., Carol Stream, Illinois 60188. All rights reserved.

Manufactured in the United States of America

ISBN 978-0-9833624-3-2

rickleland.com

Contents

Contents

Psalm 110:3 says, "Your people will volunteer freely in the day of Your power."

To You Jesus

To Your volunteers

I. Jump

"**J**ump."

Malachi Marble snugged the hood of his buckskin brown Carhartt coat as he peered out over Lake Michigan. His eyes fixed on the spot where the water turned from blue to black.

"Jump." This time, the voice in his head sounded more demanding. "Go ahead, jump."

The bluff where Malachi stood hung three stories above the water's edge. A worn switchback path off to the left descended to the shore, skirting a sizeable outcropping of rocks and stones as it neared the beach.

Eight and a half months earlier, when he first stood at this spot, the grandeur of the beauty engulfed him.

Today, the first day of 2011, the blackness of the churning water was a vivid reflection of his inner turmoil.

Jesus at Walmart...the Cost

He shook his head as he slowly said to himself, "Pastor Malachi Marble." He shivered. But it wasn't the cold. Shaking his head again, he said, "Malachi—Walmart Stocker. Department 13."

The wind blew against his face. Brisk, but not frigid. And deep inside, he knew he had an admiration for the position of a Walmart stocker. He was sure God could do mighty works through his life right where he was, job-wise, maybe even more than if he worked for a church. But now, with what had happened at the end of his shift at Walmart, it was an all-out punching match in his soul to hold onto even a remnant of that conviction.

And this morning, as the day reached toward its full illumination, Malachi's thoughts grew darker as he retraced his journey from being an Associate Pastor at St. Amos Community Church to his present job as a third shift Walmart stocker.

It started on what seemed like a normal Monday. Mattie, the receptionist, had coffee brewing, and Malachi was expecting a low-key day in his church office.

The phone rang, and from there, Malachi's life rolled downhill—rapidly. The police officer on the other end informed him they were prepared to bust down the door of Senior Pastor Neal Renner's residence—the parsonage adjacent to the church. Malachi instantly knew it was due to the pastor's involvement with marijuana. Six weeks earlier, he had smelled it at the church and knew it was Pastor Renner. But he hadn't talked to anyone about his discovery.

Malachi's attempted intervention at the parsonage, and subsequently with Pastor Renner, over the course of the next few days backfired. Malachi admitted he had approached the situation lacking some sound judgment on his part.

The backlash of attacks against Malachi pressed him to the edge. Pastor Renner, many of the elders, and even his wife,

Jump

Annie, sided against him. Still, the most vicious assault was Malachi himself—his insecurities and relived failures, while his unrealistic idealization of ministry and life chipped in its share of chaotic thinking. All this aided his now swift and significant erosion of his once vibrant relationship with God.

His marriage of fourteen years, which was already riding treacherous waves, offered no shelter. Instead, it provoked the toppling of his fragile life.

And then there was Malachi's *gift* from God—dreams, visions, impressions, and inklings, which revealed to him the unknown. He had many times asked God, "Why do You give me these dreams and…I don't know…these visions and things?" Through them, he repeatedly knew things he wished he didn't know.

At times, Malachi was perplexed. He couldn't always reconcile what God would reveal supernaturally with the things he perceived with his natural mind.

He struggled and would question, "God, how can I figure out, how can I understand the parts you don't show me?"

Leaning mainly on confusion and self-preservation as a catalyst, Malachi ran from his ministry job, his marriage, and even God.

Hoping to get a job in construction, working for his Uncle Dale Marble in Manistee, Michigan, Malachi trekked seven hours north without telling anyone, even keeping it a secret from his uncle.

Malachi ended up on the bottom rung of life when he found out that Uncle Dale's job offer no longer stood. Instead, Uncle Dale was battling cancer and was nearly broke.

Even as gloom descended on the evening of these discoveries, Malachi met Mandy Howard, a waitress at a downtown Manistee restaurant where he dined with Uncle Dale. She became a bit of a glimmer in his despair.

Fueled by desperation and Uncle Dale's working

relationship with one of the managers, Malachi secured a job at Walmart. And soon found a *home* at a remote campsite overlooking Turquoise Bottom Creek located in the vast Manistee National Forest.

Malachi blinked. He thought to himself, "2011. A new year. God, please let things be better this year. God…please."

He rubbed the side of his face and said quietly, "I thought I was over all that…all this…mess. I thought I had broken through to freedom. Now these thoughts, these feelings. Oh God, they've been stirred up again."

He glanced at his watch. 8:17. A little over an hour ago, he had completed his late-night shift at Walmart. There was little acknowledgement among the workers that a new year had arrived. No celebration for a hope-filled year, and no resolutions pointing to a better life. Just arduous work as the crew pressed hard to the end of the shift.

While some of his coworkers were going to celebrate—to party, Malachi wanted to be alone.

Alone to evaluate life. Alone to evaluate the meaning of a new year. Alone to toil against another round of inner craziness. And just maybe, alone to sense God in a special way.

Now, all he was doing was fighting the thoughts that were bombarding his brain. A battle with an unseen adversary.

"Jump Malachi."

"I'm not going to jump."

"What if this year is worse than last year? You know it's going to be."

"You're wrong. Just go away."

"You and Annie, the Jesus at Walmart Bible study, you and Mandy—failures. And Stu. Awful failures. How long are you going to work at Walmart? You think you're a pastor…of what? It's too much. How much more can you suffer? The cost to endure any further is just too much."

Jump

"I wouldn't die if I landed on those rocks. I would probably be paralyzed or in a coma or something…."

"Since you're thinking about ending your pain—all you need is a better way. And then there would be no more pain. Just freedom. No Annie. No Mandy. No Walmart. Only freedom."

Malachi fixed his gaze again out over the distant water—the place where blue water turned into a blackish abyss. He shook his head after several moments of silence. And then he said in a barely audible voice, "Freedom."

"That's right—freedom. Just jump. Why not end it all? It's hopeless. Malachi, you can do it painlessly. You could get a gun. Just like…"

"You jump devil! You jump!" Malachi shrieked out over the vast expanse. "You jump!"

2. A Friend

Malachi spun his body abruptly around, like a soldier performing an about face.

"Crap," he said. "I mean…," as he stood eyeball to eyeball with Carl—his best friend.

Malachi's body didn't move, but his mind traveled lightspeed through his memory banks.

Carl. Carl Lacombe. They had met at this very spot the day after Malachi had arrived in Manistee. Following their initial encounter, one word defined Malachi's opinion of Carl—kook.

Despite some bizarre, unexplainable incidences over the next few weeks, the ever-pleasant Carl chipped away at Malachi's skepticism. The melt culminated, when he pressed

Malachi to attend a church service—through much resistance. And Malachi experienced God like never before.

Because of what happened that night, Malachi later told Carl, "You saved my life."

He replied, "No…Jesus saved your life, Malachi, not me."

Carl was an ex-hippy who found Jesus unexpectedly at a California McDonald's in 1967 during an early wave of the Jesus Movement.

While Carl intentionally avoided the label, many Godly people had described him as gifted in the prophetic. Very gifted.

He was always concerned about the misunderstandings he would have to overcome if he wore the *prophetically gifted* tag. He simply said of himself, "For some reason, I seem to hear the voice of God much more pronounced than most followers of Jesus. My overarching objective is to obey God. If He reveals a situation He wants me involved in, my desire is to honor Him with my response."

He had traveled extensively for twenty years serving in ministry, using his gifting. Eventually, sin among the organization's leaders began to devour the ministry he was working with, so Carl made a stand against those involved in the ungodly behavior. And lost.

He told Malachi, "I was marked as a heretic…everything I was from the moment I became a Jesus follower was ripped away in a couple of days. I nearly gave up on God. It was so difficult to trust God…to trust Him at all. My life was horrible; I considered suicide."

Through all, he had persevered. And Carl had been waiting years for God to use him again in ministry. Essentially, as he put it, "God's been refining me…on the backside of the desert."

And then Carl met Malachi…

A Friend

Malachi's heart was throbbing as if he had just finished a 100-yard dash. He drew in a deep breath before he said, "What are you doing here?"

"You know how God talks to me?" Carl said. "I heard that one of His sheep needed rescuing."

Malachi dropped his eyes toward the ground. And then raised his head after a few seconds, looking Carl directly in the eyes. He forced a half-smile on his face, "Yeah. Yeah…that would be me."

Carl clutched Malachi in an embrace and then said, "Do you want to go get some coffee?"

"No…ah…let's just stay here. I'll warm up the Suburban."

3. Warmth in a Rusty Suburban

They walked the forty paces from the bluff overlooking Lake Michigan to the parking area.

"The Suburban warms up fast," Malachi said. "Go ahead and hop in."

Several seconds of silence followed the sound of doors closing. They sat in the prolonged stillness long after they had both settled into their seats. Malachi thought to himself, "True friends are comfortable when no one is speaking."

The muffler rumbled. Not a pleasant dually reverb. More like, "Fix me. Replace me." And if the body of the Suburban could speak, it would be saying, "Help, the rust is eating me up." Money, time, and lack of motivation forced the Suburban to fend for itself. Yet, to Malachi, the vehicle was more than just a ride; it was a trusty friend—rust and all.

"I'm a wimp," Malachi said. "Carl, why am I so fragile, so weak for God?"

"God has chosen the weak things of the world to put to shame the things which are mighty," Carl said.

"So, what am I doing wrong? I'm not putting anything mighty to shame," Malachi said as he glanced at Carl and then glared straight ahead.

Malachi looked over at Carl again.

Three of Carl's fingers stroked his lower lip. He stared at the windshield. His drawn-out wordlessness began to disquiet Malachi, like a lover searching the mailbox for a letter that hadn't arrived.

"Say something, Carl."

"You're the one who needs to talk," he said as he turned and looked directly at Malachi.

"Are you warm enough?" Malachi said.

"Yeah. This thing really blasts out the heat."

"I'll turn the heat down."

Malachi drew in a few slow breaths through his nose. He interlocked his fingers, rubbing them back and forth. "Remember that church service at Become Ministries when God gave me the idea for Jesus at Walmart?"

The words on the sign outside of the church beamed into Malachi's brain. His mind relived that evening from months prior.

Become Ministries—Become Lovers of Jesus, Become God's Servant, Become Sensitive to the Holy Spirit, Become the Person God Gifted You to Be.

The music, the praises to God, caused Malachi to sense His presence—His nearness. Malachi's heart was straining with thankfulness to God. His parched spirit was undergoing rejuvenation.

Tears came repeatedly to his eyes before the end of the

singing and Pastor Jonathan's first words.

"Turn with me tonight in your Bibles to Isaiah 6 and let me read what's probably the most familiar passage in all of Isaiah; we all know it. 'Whom shall I send and who will go for Us?' And we know Isaiah responded, 'Here am I. Send me!'"

Pastor Jonathan stepped down from the platform and began moving back and forth, "Friends, a few verses earlier, Isaiah had the type of experience that we call around here, 'A mighty time in the Lord.' The kind of experience that will change your life forever. Though sometimes challenging, for us, the Presence of God during these experiences just feels so good. But now, God is sending Isaiah to go tell the people. And in a parallel fashion, I hear God telling us—out, out, out, get out of the church."

Pastor Jonathan proclaimed the need for followers of Jesus to get outside of the church. "Friends, we need to send you. Imprint a big Holy Ghost stamp on you. Get the address of where God wants you to go inscribed on your heart. And out you all go as letters—proclaiming the Good News of Jesus Christ. Friends, people need Jesus at school, people need Jesus at your workplace, people need Jesus at McDonalds, people need Jesus at Walmart…"

When Malachi heard, "People need Jesus at Walmart," he felt like jumping up and power punching the air, "Yes!"

And then twenty-five minutes later, Malachi told Carl, "I'm going to start a Jesus-group at Walmart, a Bible study, more than a Bible study."

Carl looked at Malachi and smiled, "That was quite a church service. I'm still in awe of God for giving you the idea to start Jesus at Walmart that night. It doesn't seem like six months ago. The memory is still so vivid."

"Actually, it's been over seven months," Malachi said.

Malachi shifted his focus to the left and looked intently

out the side window. "And then only a few weeks later, God opened the door for the first Jesus at Walmart meeting. I had…just…just such high expectations."

He continued to gaze out the side window as his mind momentarily drifted back again.

Everything was ready for the first meeting. Chairs arranged in the Walmart conference room. Bibles and handouts awaiting attendees. At 3:00 A.M. there was no one there besides Malachi. Reasons bounced around inside Malachi's head. And then at 3:06, Carl and Mandy showed up.

Malachi looked at Carl. "Forgive me for rambling on; my mind is drifting," he said.

"Help me, Carl. I need some help here."

"You're doing fine," Carl said. "You ever notice in the Psalms that David voiced his share of angst, pain, and disappointments?"

"Yeah. But that's not really helping me with the fact that not even one Walmart employee showed up at the first meeting. Sure, you and a waitress from a local restaurant attended. But Jesus at Walmart has struggled to keep any consistent momentum since then. Well, actually, it's just flat out faltered."

"I think Mandy was more than a waitress to you. You were falling in love with her."

"But then you…"

"You mean God…"

"Yeah, you were right. God was right. I should have never gone out on a date with her," Malachi said. "But I sure…I sure…" He shook his head. "But that was the past."

"God has chosen the weak things of the world to put to shame the things which are mighty," Carl said again. "Malachi, you're trying to be mighty by your own standards. Everybody wants to be the Jesus superhero type. I think God's actually looking for some good old-fashioned trench diggers, who will just do what He asks. One shovel and then another. People who will shovel and shovel. Workers who don't have to hit gold every other scoop. God needs people who are *doing the stuff.*"

"You're right," Malachi said. And then like an abrupt U-turn, he said, "I sure love Mandy."

Carl cocked his head, followed by a nod, "Yeah, I know."

"Do you remember the question she asked me at that first Jesus at Walmart meeting?" Malachi said.

"Let me think. Yeah," Carl said. "Let's see…God guided you to have Mandy read Psalm 37:4, 'Delight yourself in the Lord and He will give you the desires of your heart.'" He paused, "And then…then…she asked, 'What does that mean?'"

"Carl, is that moment etched in your mind like it is mine?"

4. God Will Give You the Desires of Your Heart?

Malachi's delight fluttered like a reed blowing in the wind as his eyes absorbed the pleasure of seeing Mandy's fingers cradling God's Word, so much so that he had to prod himself back to the moment. "Mandy can you read Psalm 37:4? Father God has something He wants to tell you."

She bowed her head toward the Bible as she spoke the words, "Delight yourself in the Lord and He will give you the desires of your heart."

Several seconds of silence sounded before Mandy looked up—straight at Malachi and said, "What does that mean?"

"What are the desires of your heart, Mandy? Deep inside, what do you really want? Really, really want?" Malachi said.

"I guess…well…I want a perfect life."

Malachi glanced at Carl and then shifted his focus back to

Mandy. He grinned. "You want it all. Don't you?"

"Well sure," she said. "Is that what God will do for me?"

Malachi paused for a couple of seconds, turning his eyes to Carl and then back to Mandy. "If you have enough money, will life be perfect? That would be nice. But we all know it doesn't work that way. Face it, rich does not equal happy. We want to have perfect people around us. Will that give us the perfect life?"

"Huh…perfect people?" Mandy said.

Malachi shook his head, "Exactly. God, as one of the ways He expresses His love, allows every human to make the choice of how they will act. And we never make all the right choices. Do we? Self-interest seems to drive us too much of the time. You know, 'Get out of my way. It's all about me.' Have you ever seen that at work, Mandy? Down at DT's Good Time Place?"

"No never."

They all laughed.

"I could go on and on," Malachi said. "The perfect job. Or how about the perfect buzz from the perfect beer? How many Trinity Darks do you need to drink to get there?"

Then Malachi picked up his Bible with both hands. "The answer to truly knowing our own heart, even knowing what to desire and to…" Malachi paused, "Perfection is…ah…"

He shifted his eyes toward his Bible, "Let me read Psalm 37:4 again, and then I'll read the following verse also. 'Delight yourself in the Lord and He will give you the desires of your heart. Commit your way to the Lord, trust also in Him, and He will do it.'"

He directed his attention to Mandy again. "Here's a way to explain all this. Someone comes into DT's. They look at the menu and delight in one of the food items. They're thinking, 'This is going to be really tasty. It's going to fill my tummy nicely. Yum, yum.' The desire for the food item rises and becomes a desire of their heart—'I've got to have it.' But delight plus desire does not equal a plate of food on the table. Commit—that's what comes next. When a person places the order, they are committing to paying the cost. No commitment; no food; no desire of the heart. Part of the commitment to paying the cost is that I trust the food will arrive. And I'm trusting that it will fulfill the desire of my heart. The food will do it. God will do it. God will give us the desires of our heart as we commit to Him and His ways. And trusting Him with all our heart that He—God will do it. Is this making any sense, Mandy?"

She nodded her head and said slowly, "Yeah. Yeah. I'm seeing the connection, Malachi. It's like if my son, Alex, really wants something, he has to do what I tell him he needs to do to get it. And when he does what I say, he trusts that I will do what I said I would. Alex trusts that I will do it."

Malachi tilted his head slightly. His eyes were on Mandy, and then he looked over at Carl, "Wow, she really gets it."

Mandy grinned.

Malachi glanced at his watch, "Oh, I've got to get back to work. But…ah let me just say, this whole package can never fully come together in our lives until we have made the ultimate connection with Jesus Christ."

He then stood up, "Sorry…got to get back to stocking." He lightly embraced Mandy, "Thank you so much for coming tonight. Thank you. Please come back next week. O.K.?"

Mandy smiled. "Yeah. I will."

Malachi hugged Carl. "You're the best."

5. Commit. Trust.
Will He Do It?

"I'll walk you back to the time clock," Carl said. "I want to read you something."

"Sure," Malachi said.

"This is from 2 Corinthians 4:7-17," Carl said. And then he began to read:

> We have this treasure in earthen vessels, so that the surpassing greatness of the power will be of God and not from ourselves. We are afflicted in every way, but not crushed. Perplexed, but not despairing. Persecuted, but not forsaken. Struck down, but not destroyed. Always carrying about in the body, the dying of Jesus. So that the life of Jesus also may be manifested in our body.

For we who live are constantly being delivered over to death for Jesus' sake, so that the life of Jesus also may be manifested in our mortal flesh. So, death works in us, but life in you.

But having the same spirit of faith, according to what is written, 'I believe; therefore, I spoke,' we also believe, therefore we also speak, knowing that He who raised the Lord Jesus will raise us also with Jesus and will present us with you.

For all things are for your sake, so that the grace which is spreading to more and more people may cause the giving of thanks to abound to the glory of God.

Therefore we do not lose heart, but though our outer man is decaying, yet our inner man is being renewed day by day. For momentary, light affliction is producing for us an eternal weight of glory far beyond all comparison.

After he had finished, Carl looked at Malachi with an uncharacteristically, somber expression.

"Well...thank you Carl," Malachi said. "Is there something you want me to know?"

"It's always good to be prepared," Carl said.

Malachi cocked his head to the right and furrowed his brow, "Prepared?"

Carl's gaze washed over Malachi. "You did an excellent job tonight. Our Father was very pleased."

"Hey Malachi," someone said.

He turned to look. It was Stu.

"Carl, thanks for everything," Malachi said. "See you soon."

"Hey Stu," Malachi said. "What's up?"

"Let's talk on our way back to our departments," Stu said. "We still have a lot of freight to get on the shelves tonight."

"Sure," Malachi said. "I was thinking you would show up at the first Jesus at Walmart."

Commit. Trust. Will He Do It?

"Long story," Stu said. "Sorry I couldn't make it."

Stu—the store evangelist.

Twenty minutes after they had met for the first time, Stu said, "...do you know Jesus?" A bold witness for Jesus—though often an irritating contrarian in the spiritual arena. He also carried the nickname *The Finisher*, because he was by far the store's fastest stocker, and he would always jump in to help other associates finish stocking their shelves.

And then there was the side of Stu that gripped Malachi. He was prone to running amok—sliding back into his pre-Jesus lifestyle, so much so that Malachi would have distress regarding his survival.

They walked side by side toward the departments they stocked. Malachi was heading to Chemicals and Stu was going to Paper Goods.

"So, what did you want, Stu?"

He stopped and looked intently at Malachi. "I really need your help. I'm desperate. Can you help me?"

"Sure Stu. What...ah...what is it?"

"We have to talk at break."

"You got it. I'll see you in the break room."

"No. Not in the break room. Outside. Please. I need you, Malachi. I'm desperate...please, Malachi. I need your help. O.K.?"

Malachi put his hand on Stu's shoulder. "Everything's going to be alright. Outside is fine."

"You're a true friend," Stu said. "Thank you, Malachi... so much."

Malachi shifted his focus to stocking the shelves and thought, "I've never seen Stu this frenzied, this agitated at work."

When break time arrived, Stu was prompt, "You ready, Malachi? I need your help. This will only take a few minutes."

They hurried through the southerly set of doors.

Once outside, Stu pointed to the north section of the parking lot. "We need to go over to my car."

The thought quickly entered Malachi's mind, "All the associates park in the south section of the parking lot." But the seeming gravity of the situation didn't allow him to ponder the discrepancy. And tonight, in that section of the parking lot, two cars were parked near each other.

Stu was striding briskly as they made their way to his car. He opened the door and whipped out a knife.

Even with the moderate illumination cascading from overhead, Malachi could see the knife's details. Nearly a foot long, the blade was black steel. The last few inches of the upper edge of the blade curved down to meet the upswinging curve of the lower one. Both had chisel sharp edges. The handle was pearl white with intermittent black bands.

Malachi sucked air in hard when he saw it. His heart raced. Though he didn't feel threatened because Stu was cradling the blade. "Here, take the knife, Malachi. I've been having awful thoughts about ending my own…"

"Stu!" Malachi said as he took the knife.

Seconds after he had a sure grip on the knife's handle, the full force of Stu's right fist pummeled Malachi's wrist. The knife hit the pavement with a clang. Instantly, Stu smashed into Malachi as if he was a tackle-dummy.

"What…" Malachi screamed as his body bounced hard against the asphalt.

With all his power, Stu pinned Malachi to the ground.

He jerked Malachi's left arm around his body, pinning it to his back, and forced his face against the abrasive blacktop.

Malachi quickly gave up struggling, knowing the futility.

And then he heard someone say, "I'll call the police."

He recognized the voice. It was Burt Gunner—the store manager.

Malachi wondered why Stu didn't flee. Instead, he intensified the pressure when Malachi said, "Stu let…"

So, he laid there—steeped in thought as he waited for the police to arrive.

Malachi's thoughts traveled back to earlier in the shift, when he was waiting for people to arrive at Jesus at Walmart—at 2:55, Malachi had noticed movement near the door. It was Burt Gunner—he passed by the door, heading into the store. This perplexed Malachi because Burt rarely, if ever, came to the store during the overnight shift. Malachi had said to himself, "What's he doing here tonight…?"

Now with his face rubbing against the cold hard surface, he said just above a whisper, "Thank you God." He mused at the irony of how God was working things out.

Burt had been Malachi's biggest and only opposition to Jesus at Walmart, so much so that he had concocted a plan to get Malachi terminated—ending all his ministry aspirations at the store. Burt's plans were thwarted when God gave Malachi some *intense impressions* regarding Burt's past behavior at Walmart. Behavior that would be devastating to his career and livelihood. Burt backed down, and Jesus at Walmart prevailed.

And now, God was even using Burt, a former foe, as the rescuing hero, even though Malachi sensed anguish because he knew Stu was going to have to face the consequences of his bizarre behavior.

The police car sirens were sounding. And in moments, Malachi heard a car skid to an abrupt stop. A door slammed and a voice said, "What's going on here?"

"The man Stu apprehended pulled a knife on me," Burt said. "He is an associate here. A troublemaker. The knife is laying there on the ground."

"He's involved in a cult," Stu said as the officer pulled Malachi's hands behind his back and slapped handcuffs on his wrists. "And he planned on spreading the cult plague to Walmarts all over the country. Burt caught him."

"That's not true," Malachi said as he was raised to his feet, pressed against the hood of the police car, and padded down. "This is a church type group. A Bible study. It's about Jesus."

"That's what all cult leaders say," the officer replied. Then he barked, "Be quiet. Listen up: this is the legal deal—You have the right to remain silent. Anything you say or do can and will be held against you in a court of law. You have the right to an attorney. If you cannot afford an attorney, one will be appointed for you. Do you understand each of these rights I have explained to you?"

"But I didn't…" Malachi said.

"Hey!" the officer said. "Answer the question. And here's my advice—zip it. You'll get your say. Now! Just answer. Do you understand your rights?"

"Yes sir…I do."

The officer escorted Malachi to the squad car and placed him in the rear seat. After slamming the door shut, he returned to talk with Burt.

Malachi positioned his ear against the cold glass of the side window and was able to hear the muted sound of their conversation.

"I was called in tonight because someone had clandestinely disabled our parking lot security cameras," Burt said. "We were not able to fix them—not till morning." He then looked toward Malachi. "I think we know the culprit."

"God help me," Malachi prayed.

As he peered out the window, everything seemed surreal. His whirling mind couldn't fully comprehend what was going on. It was like trying to read a book with all the vowels removed from the words.

He shook his head as he looked up into the black sky. "God, what's going on?"

6. Momentary, Light Affliction is...

"'Therefore we do not lose heart, but though our outer man is decaying, yet our inner man is being renewed day by day. For momentary, light affliction is producing for us an eternal weight of glory far beyond all comparison.' 2 Corinthians 4:16 and 17." Malachi said.

He switched the Suburban's heater to defrost to clear the windshield and then shifted his body as he looked at Carl. "When you read those scriptures to me, I never realized how much I would need them. I never told you this. So many things started happening...we just never talked about it. And of all those scriptures that you had read to me a couple of hours before I was arrested, I had those two memorized."

Carl nodded.

"When I was riding in the police car, my own thoughts

were assaulting me. The only relief I could find was to focus on those verses," Malachi said. "Carl, why did you give me those Bible verses? I never asked you. Did you know what was going to happen to me that night in the parking lot?"

"God stirred my heart like He had the first time we met," Carl said. "Right here at this park when you first came to Manistee. You remember that day, Malachi?"

"I'm sure I'll remember it the rest of my life," Malachi said as his gaze shifted out through the windshield to the very spot they had first met.

...that day, Malachi scanned out to where the sky touches the water—engulfed in the grandeur of the beauty.

"Are you finding what you're looking for?" Carl had said.

Then Malachi whipped around to see a stranger.

A lanky man, Carl, was scrutinizing Malachi. And grinning at him at the same time. His thinning, mostly brown hair was short and windblown. Besides his cockeyed smile, Malachi noticed a dancing sparkle in his eyes.

The question passed through his mind, "Is this drug or alcohol induced?"

"Did I scare you?" the man, who appeared to be around seventy, asked.

"Ah...you startled me. Where did you come from?"

"I asked the first question. Are you finding what you're looking for? You look a little lost."

"He's dressed a notch too nice for a bum," Malachi surmised. "Still?"

"I don't know," Malachi said. "I don't even know what I'm looking for."

Turning back toward Lake Michigan, his eyes fixed again on the far away line where dark-blue water danced with bright-blue sky.

"Do you think you can hide from God?" the man said.

Malachi spun around. "I'm through with God! …who are you?"

"But is God through with you?"

"Who are you," Malachi asked a second time.

"Does it matter who I am?"

The old man then put on a pair of sunglasses—cheap looking, oversized, black-framed, toy-like glasses. And walked to the edge of the bluff. After taking a few steps on the switchback leading to the beach, he stopped, and turned around. "Maybe you should get a job at Walmart."

"Like that day eight months ago, Malachi, God sometimes gives me strong impressions, sometimes to the degree that I'm seeing pictures," Carl said. "It's like He's giving me an assignment—because He is. But all I know is my part. I rarely…well let me think…I should say…I essentially never see *the why, the end result*. Sure, often through observation and just thinking the situation over, I know what's going on. But many times, I'm clueless beyond my part. It's very unnerving…that doesn't sound very faith-filled, very Godly, but…still my objective is to obey God."

"So, you read me some Bible verses—assignment complete. And off you go singing, 'Tis so sweet to trust in Jesus,' as Stu sands the parking lot with my face—trying to break my arm off."

Carl chuckled. "Pretty much."

"That's comforting."

"Malachi, you know the Bible says the Holy Spirit is our Comforter. Too many people want other people to be their *comforter*. I'm talking Believers—clinging to other Believers for their comfort…for their…for almost everything. Instead of God. Instead of the Holy Spirit."

"Yeah. I know…" Malachi said.

"Spiritual shop-vacs sucking the life out of other people,"

Carl said. "Do this for me. Do that for me. I remember once someone wanted me to pray for them. This person said, 'I was wishing, hoping, and praying,' as his life was mired in destruction. Actually, all they were doing was wishing. *Wishing, wishing, wishing.* I said, 'You need to do something besides just wishing.' And then I laid out three baby steps to help nudge that person in a Godly direction."

"How'd that work?"

"Never saw him again. He latched on to someone else, like a spiritual shop-vac."

"Yeah. That's for sure."

"Another time, there was this guy who came to me who had a serious lust problem. His marriage was on the edge. When he sinned, he always claimed he was getting better. And then he would quote Jesus to himself, 'Be of good cheer I have overcome the world.' Now this guy wasn't overcoming his problem, but he thought he should be of *good cheer*—and I'm not even sure why he thought that. I mean...should you ever be of good cheer when you sin?"

Malachi laughed.

"Again, I gave him some practical, Biblical steps toward freedom. You know what he said to me? 'Can't you pray that God will just set me free?' I stared at him. Then he said, 'Don't you have enough power?' He wasn't willing to take even one step. Another spiritual shop-vac."

"Yeah, it's sad when people are that way," Malachi said.

Carl shifted in his seat, looking directly at Malachi. "Can you think of anyone else who might be spiritual shop-vacish?"

Malachi looked away, shifting his eyes downward, and was silent for a few moments. And then raised his head, "I guess...ah...landing in jail, even for the wrong reason, isn't a good enough excuse for sucking."

Carl tilted his head as a smirk came across his face, "Tis so sweet to trust in Jesus."

7. Tis So Sweet to Trust in Jesus

Malachi thought to himself as he heard the barred door close, "That sounds exactly like it does in the movies." The clanging echo faded as he made his way to his single cot.

He looked around his cell—everything appeared to be gray. Gray, gray. The closely spaced one-inch round-bars interspersed every sixteen inches with three quarter-inch flat steel running horizontally were gray. The concrete floor was gray. The three inner walls constructed of standard concrete blocks were gray. Though he did notice that the conduit running to the steel-cage domed light fixtures, the size of a quart jar, were a darker shade of gray. Even the heavy-duty welded angle iron bed frame was gray. Gray, gray. And it appeared to be anchored to the floor—the gray floor.

There was another cot in the cell. It was unoccupied. Down

the corridor, Malachi had noticed one other cell adjacent to his. He assumed it was identical. In the corner of Malachi's cell was a white porcelain toilet stool—out in the open. And a sink anchored to the wall hung eight inches to the left of it.

Malachi sat on the edge of his bed, looking at the residue of ink on his fingers. Adrenaline was still coursing through his body—sleep would be impossible.

He thought, "This seems like a scene from a movie. O.K., so what's next?"

His brain was being bombarded by thoughts and pictures.

He noticed the pain in his right wrist as the scene of Stu bashing the knife to the ground flashed in his mind. And then feelings of rage fouled his mood, when scenes of seeing Burt through the squad car window flickered inside his head. Like trying to erase a chalkboard with a Q-tip, he attempted to smear the anger away. Malachi shook his head back and forth several times in an effort to dislodge his fury.

It seemed to work. A smile tried to form on his face as his imagination drew a bead on Mandy's expression during the Jesus at Walmart meeting. The moment when she had said, "What does that mean?" She was asking, "What does, 'Delight yourself in the Lord and He will give you the desires of your heart,' mean?"

He smiled. "I love Mandy. I adore her childlike reaching toward God. Thank you, God."

The two Bible verses they discussed surfaced in Malachi's mind: "Delight yourself in the Lord and He will give you the desires of your heart. Commit your way to the Lord, trust also in Him, and He will do it."

"Crap," Malachi said to himself. "I commit. I trust. I try my best to delight in You God. And now another desire of my heart is gone; Jesus at Walmart is finished after only one meeting…"

He stared at the concrete floor. In the solitude, he could

hear his own breathing. And then he inspected the ink stains on his fingers once again. As if they might reveal some clues for his plight.

His sigh was audible.

Words of David from the book of Psalms started to trickle into his mind:

> Why are you in despair, O my soul? And why have you become disturbed within me? Hope in God, for I shall again praise Him for the help of His presence.
>
> O my God, my soul is in despair within me… Deep calls to deep…all Your breakers and Your waves have rolled over me.
>
> The Lord will command His lovingkindness in the daytime. And His song will be with me in the night. I will say to God my Rock, 'Why have You forgotten me? Why do I go mourning because of the oppression of the enemy?'
>
> As a shattering of my bones, my adversaries revile me. While they say to me all day long, 'Where is your God?' Why are you in despair, O my soul?
>
> O my soul.
>
> O my soul.
>
> O my soul.
>
> …O my soul.

"Why are you in despair, O my soul?"

"Why?"

And then Malachi turned his head as he tilted his right ear toward the bars. He thought, "What is…is that…a radio? Is someone singing? I know that song."

Tis so sweet to trust in Jesus

Jesus at Walmart...the Cost

Just to take Him at His Word
Just to rest upon His promise
And to know, "Thus saith the Lord"

Jesus, Jesus, how I trust Him
How I've proved Him o'er and o'er
Jesus, Jesus, precious Jesus
Oh, for grace to trust Him more

Oh, how sweet to trust in Jesus
Just to trust His cleansing blood
And in simple faith to plunge me
'Neath the healing, cleansing flood

Jesus, Jesus, how I trust Him
How I've proved Him o'er and o'er
Jesus, Jesus, precious Jesus
Oh, for grace to trust Him more

Yes 'tis sweet to trust in Jesus
Just from sin and self to cease
Just from Jesus simply taking
Life and rest, and joy and peace

Jesus, Jesus, how I trust Him
How I've proved Him o'er and o'er
Jesus, Jesus, precious Jesus
Oh, for grace to trust Him more

I'm so glad I learned to trust Thee
Precious Jesus, Savior, Friend
And I know that Thou art with me
Wilt be with me to the end

Tis So Sweet to Trust in Jesus

> Jesus, Jesus, how I trust Him
> How I've proved Him o'er and o'er
> Jesus, Jesus, precious Jesus
> Oh, for grace to trust Him more

Malachi sat silently as, "Yes, yes, yes!" started reverberating inside his soul.

And then a voice, like a whisper through a megaphone, said, "Do you know the cost?"

"What?" Malachi said. "What do you mean…the cost?"

"The cost of following Jesus?"

"I'm here in jail for Jesus…well, maybe, because I made my boss mad…but I'm here because of Jesus. Well…yeah… ah…yeah, that's why I'm here," Malachi said. "And what about you?"

Malachi waited for several seconds. And several seconds more. "Did you hear me?"

"…I said, did you hear me?"

Malachi stood up and walked to the bars, "Hey! Hello! Hey…your song…it really got to me…it ah…it touched my soul."

"Hey there. Can you hear me?"

Malachi's words echoed against the gray walls of the cell-block hallway, "Hey, thanks for the song. Are you there?"

8. A JC Thing

Another voice woke him up in the morning, "Mr. Malachi Marble."

Malachi awoke easily, even though he had slept very little all night. His mind snapped to full attention when he heard his name.

"Yes Sir."

"You've been charged with assault with intent to do great bodily harm. Bail has been set at $10,000," an officer said.

"$10,000?"

"That's right."

"Now what do I do? I've never been in jail."

"If you get a bail bondsman, $1,000 will get you out."

"$1,000," Malachi said.

"That is correct, Mr. Marble," the officer said. "Is there

someone you would like to call?"

Malachi pondered, "Uncle Dale—no he wouldn't have the money. Pastor Jonathan—I can't do that. Carl—no money. Mandy—that would be stupid. Anybody at Walmart—nope."

"Officer, I just...I ah...don't have anyone to call...right now," Malachi said. "I need...ah...I need to think this over.'"

"You can always make a call at a later time," he said. "But now, I will be moving you from the holding cell corridor over to the main cell block."

As the officer opened the cell door, Malachi looked to his right and peered into the only other cell in the corridor. He froze for a second.

"Let's go, Mr. Marble."

"Where's the man who was in the other cell last night?"

"You're the only one down here."

"How about last night?"

"You're it."

"I heard someone singing. And he talked to me," Malachi said. "Sounds must have carried through the wall."

"Through sixteen inches of solid concrete?" the officer said. "No way."

"Hold it...you're telling me..."

"You hold it, Mr. Marble!" the officer said. "Let's go. Now!"

Malachi glanced back one more time.

"Now!" the officer said as he jerked his arm.

And then they headed into the bowels of the Manistee County Jail.

As they walked the passageway, twice massive steel doors retracted into the walls and then clanged shut behind them.

Malachi was thinking, "I was too intimidated to do jail ministry. But now, here I am."

As each door rumbled closed, he felt more uneasy. "Oh God help me," he whispered to himself.

Finally, they stood facing a hinged door with a small wire

glass window a foot square. To the right was an officer's station with two dark-smoked glass windows—one panel faced the door and the other peered out into the cellblock area ahead.

The officer said into his radio, "I have the new prisoner."

There was the sound of metal on metal. And then the officer pushed the door open with his right hand.

"Mr. Marble, this is your new home." The officer glanced at a piece of paper. "You've been assigned to cell 6-C. Grab an empty bunk and get settled in. Sounds like you may be here a while."

Malachi's apprehension dropped several notches. It was nothing like he had expected. The area he was standing in was more like the basement fellowship hall for a little church. Six eight-foot long picnic-style tables ran side by side down the center of the room. He spotted a TV and a small counter with a microwave. He noticed some reading materials on the tables, and some of the men were playing cards. Off to his right, he saw a man quietly talking on a phone attached to the wall—it appeared to be a pay phone of some sort.

The officer looked at Malachi, "Behave yourself and things will go smoothly. Break the rules and you'll pay. Got it?"

"Yes sir."

Before the officer had even finished securing the door as he exited, a man at the nearest table said, "What you in for?"

"Ah well…"

"Have a seat dude," the man said.

"Sure."

"Name's Jamie Christler."

Malachi extended his hand, "Malachi Marble."

Jamie repeated his name slowly, "Malachi Marble…M and M. Hey everybody, Eminem has just arrived. So, Eminem—you rap?"

"Well…I…I did once at Walmart."

"Hey everybody, my man Eminem once played to a

sold-out crowd in the cereal aisle at Walmart. Let's hear it for him."

A few of the men clapped. One hollered, "Yeah, bring it." Followed by someone else's retort, "Eminem sucks."

"So, Eminem, what you in for? Maybe beating up Fifty Cent or your old lady. Or both, because you caught them together."

"You can just call me Malachi."

"So, what you in for Malachi?"

"Well…let's see. You want the truth?"

"I'm all about truth. We all are."

Malachi then heard some hardy responses from around the table, "Nothing but the truth… yeah, the whole truth… amen…the truth's gonna set me free."

"Well, Jamie, I'm in here for serving Jesus."

He laughed, "Yeah. Me too."

"What?"

"I got caught growing and selling Mary-Jesus-awana."

Malachi shook his head as Jamie hooted.

Then Malachi quickly said, "What time's chapel?"

"You changing the subject on me?" Jamie said. "We don't have chapel. There is a service on Sundays—usually."

"Perfect," Malachi said. "We can have chapel right here—tonight. I've got a story you won't want to miss. You've never heard anything like what happened to me."

"Chapel? I don't know about that. *Storage Wars* is on TV tonight. The marathon edition."

Someone at the table hollered, "Boo chapel." While someone else said, "Yea *Storage Wars*."

Malachi looked intently at Jamie and started rubbing above his right eye with his right hand. His face became warm on his right side. Between his ear and eye—above his cheekbone.

"What are you looking at?" Jamie said.

"Jamie, you know Kenny Thigpen. And the last time you went riding with him, your girlfriend, she was very angry. The changes she wants to see in your life are for your good. And your mother—she's a Godly woman. She's always praying for you. And you know that, because she tells you, 'James, I'm praying for you.'"

"Mom's the only one who calls me James. When she tells me she's praying for me," Jamie said. "Nobody knows that. Nobody. How did you know?"

"God knows."

He looked at Malachi with the stare of an indecisive poker player considering his next move. And then Jamie said, "You're the real deal, aren't you? Chapel? Sure. Right after supper…that would be cool."

"Malachi," Carl said.

"What…ah…yeah," Malachi said as he returned his thoughts back to the present moment.

"What do you want, Carl?"

"God was reaching out to you and allowing your supernatural gift to be active right in the middle of a big mess. A mess—at least from your perspective. And then…well other times…you…well you…"

"I turn into a spiritual shop-vac," Malachi said. "And start sucking life out of people. And too often that people is you."

"And sometimes, you turn that nasty thing on yourself," Carl said.

"What do you mean?"

"Well…basically, you simply don't recognize or acknowledge that God is using you in situations," Carl said. "Instead, when things don't go exactly as you expect, you're, 'Oh woe is me!'"

"Yeah."

"You're beating yourself up," Carl said. "You're turning

that menacing vac on yourself. And it sucks the life out of you."

"Yeah. I see."

"Don't do that to yourself," Carl said.

"Are you sure?" Malachi said.

They both laughed.

"I told you about the chapel service that night at the jail, didn't I?" Malachi said.

"I'm not sure," Carl said. "Refresh my memory."

"I settled in. Found my bunk. And sat there pondering what to talk about at chapel. Almost instantly, John 10:10 popped into my head."

"The thief does not come except to steal, and to kill, and to destroy. I have come that they may have life, and that they may have it more abundantly," Carl said.

"Yep. So, I started the meeting by telling them the story of how I ended up in jail. They loved it. And then I read John 10:10 from a Bible I had borrowed."

We found a spot down at the end of the hallway lined with the cells and sat down on the shiny white tiles. Jamie, Buck, and me. And after a few minutes, a guy by the name of Snyder joined us. He introduced himself as Snyder the Spider. He was bald and had a spider web tattooed on the top of his head.

"So how many times you guys been in jail?" Malachi said.

They all looked at each other.

Then Jamie spoke up, "Like six times."

"How about you, Snyder?" Malachi said.

"More than that."

"You, Buck?"

"Too many. Way too many."

"You guys must like it here," Malachi said. "You keep coming back."

And then Malachi repeated the Bible verse, "The thief

does not come except to steal, and to kill, and to destroy. I have come that they may have life, and that they may have it more abundantly. John 10:10."

He paused for a second before asking. "So, who's the thief?"

"We are," Snyder said.

"Hey, you all made it into the Bible," Malachi said, "as thieves."

They all laughed.

"Well, in a way, you're right, Snyder, but ah…not really," Malachi said. "The thief is the devil. He wants to destroy our lives. Steal everything from our lives—family, marriage, friends, jobs, our future. And ultimately, he wants to kill us. For him, a drug overdose will work just fine. Or a drunken crash. But in all of this mayhem, by our own choices, we join him in this destruction."

"Amen," Jamie said.

Malachi nodded at him, "You're getting it."

"And then we have the person whose entire desire for us is that we will have life and have it more abundantly," Malachi said. "So, who's this person?"

Buck raised his hand.

Malachi pointed at him.

"Jesus."

Malachi focused his gaze on each man in the group for a moment. "I'm going to say that each one of you, at some point in your life, has said a prayer to receive Jesus Christ as your Savior."

Jamie nodded his head.

Buck said, "Yeah."

And Snyder added, "Me too. More than once."

"But have you made Jesus, Lord of your life? Have you made Him the boss, supreme authority, master, owner of your life? Does Jesus call the shots in your life?" Malachi said.

All three were silent.

Malachi looked around the circle again and then pointed at himself with both of his index fingers, "Jamie, Buck, Snyder...this man, Malachi Marble, needs to make Jesus Christ the Lord of his life every day."

His eyes shifted down to the Bible in his hands.

"Listen to John 10:11," Malachi said. "I am the good shepherd. The good shepherd gives His life for the sheep."

He looked up at the men. "Sheep get the best from their shepherd when they let him be the boss—their Lord. We get the best from Our Good Shepherd, from Jesus, when we allow Him to be the Lord of our lives. Isn't it sad that too often sheep know how to flourish in life better than us humans?"

"That's pathetic," Jamie said as he shook his head. "A stupid sheep...doing better than us."

"Here's the deal—making Jesus the Lord of your life is going to cost you something," Malachi said. "You decide. Decide this very night. What's an abundant life worth to you? Who's the Lord of your life?"

Malachi slept only slightly better than the previous night. Rest was intermittent. At one point, he said to himself, "They sure could use some pillow-top mattresses in here. I don't think these things actually qualify as mattresses."

Then other times, he stared into the darkness—with thoughts rumbling around inside his head.

"Shouldn't I be praising God?"

"Singing or something...wouldn't that help?"

"Oh God, I just need You.

"God help me."

"Please God, help me."

When morning arrived, as everyone was going about their morning duties, Malachi heard over the loudspeaker, "Malachi Marble report to the door. Bring your personal items."

As he headed for the door, Jamie came up to him. He

rubbed his right eye with his right hand. "Hey, thanks man. Me…" He pointed his index finger upward. "Me and the Lord…I mean me and my Lord, we had a long talk last night. A real long talk."

Jamie swallowed hard. "What you said last night burned a hole in my soul. I never saw things that way before."

He reached out and embraced Malachi. "The Lord be with you, Malachi."

"And also with you, Jamie."

An officer stood at the open door. "Malachi Marble."

"Yes sir."

"You ready to go? You've been bailed out."

"Really? Wow. I'm amazed," Malachi said. Then he looked upward, "Thank You God!"

9. Malachi, Come Home with Me

"**C**arl, when the officer said, 'You've been bailed out,' your face came to mind," Malachi said.

"Seems God had a different plan," Carl said.

"Yeah. Kind of…I don't know."

"What do you mean?"

"Of course, I was praising God because I was getting out of jail, expecting to see you. But when I saw JC, I ah…it just popped into my head…I couldn't help it. I thought, 'Crap.'"

Carl scrunched his face, "Why's that, Malachi?"

"I never told you about some of the conversations I had with her."

"I don't actually ever remember you talking about JC back then."

"Well, this is what happened a few nights after I started at

Walmart. I think it was the second night..."

Only two people were in the break room, JC and someone Malachi didn't know—at least by name. JC, at a table alone, appeared to be sleeping.

He walked quietly past her and inserted his money into a vending machine. Click. Clunk. And he had his Coke.

Malachi made his way toward a vacant table.

As he prepared to sit down he heard, "Too good to sit at my table." He recognized JC's hint-of-southern voice.

So, he went over and sat across from her.

"I thought you were sleeping. I didn't want to disturb you."

"Well, maybe I was dreaming about you." She didn't smile. She already was.

Malachi felt his heart beating faster, especially after JC's foot bumped his under the table.

"So where do you live, Malachi?" JC said.

"I just moved to the area. It's a long story."

"There are a lot of long stories around here."

"Yeah. I've got a long story," Malachi said.

"If you ever want to talk after work sometime, let me know." She was still smiling.

"Carl, don't get me wrong. JC was always a nice person. But she was...ah...she was..."

"She was seductive," Carl said.

"Yeah," Malachi said. "And to be flat-out honest, especially with leaving Annie and all the upheaval in my life, I just wanted to cuddle up with someone...well more than that...you know what I mean, Carl. I had to fight some urges, because the flirting was ongoing."

"The Proverbs 5 woman," Carl said. "For the lips of an adulterous woman drip honey and smoother than oil is her speech. But in the end she is bitter as wormwood. Sharp as a two-edged sword."

"But there was another side to JC, because another time…"

Malachi and JC strolled to the least congested part of the store.

"I really like working with you, JC. You're such a hard worker. And you're funny…well not exactly funny… ah, when you're…ah…this isn't going very good."

He stopped walking and turned to look directly at JC. "I don't want to hurt your feelings. I mean…oh maybe we should just talk another time."

"Malachi, just say it. O.K.," JC said.

"JC, I don't want our friendship to be about flirting. I could be misconstruing your behavior, and if I am, forgive me. I ah…"

"It's my fault. I flirt—it's like a bad habit," JC said. "And it gets me in trouble."

"JC, you're special in God's eyes. There's something missing in your life. You keep trying to fill it up with the wrong thing. You've never experienced pure love. You try to earn love. Deep inside, you don't think you're worthy of love. Lots of people feel the same way. That's what God is all about—God is love. Do you want to experience pure love—love you don't have to earn? Love that flows when you're convinced you don't deserve it. Love that finds us when we deserve it the least."

JC looked up. "I must be feeling that love right now."

"That's the love of Jesus. You need His love in your life."

Malachi glanced at his watch. "Do you want to talk at lunch?"

"I need to be alone—to sort some things out."

"I know what you mean. Take God with you. We can talk another time. Even after work…we can talk about God."

"Yeah…maybe we should."

"You know, Carl, when JC didn't show up for that first Jesus at Walmart meeting, it bothered me a lot. I was almost positive she would be there."

"Well, we know the reason now."

"But not at the time," Malachi said. "Still, can you imagine how uneasy I felt the moment I saw JC at the Police Department, the second when her first words struck my brain?"

"Malachi, you can come home with me," JC said as they embraced in what Malachi considered an unavoidable hug.

Malachi pulled back and looked directly at her. "No. JC, I can't do that."

"Why not?" she said.

"It ah…," Malachi said. "It just wouldn't be right. You know what I mean."

JC looked down at the floor and then returned her focus to Malachi. "I want to do something good, something right… for a change. Even I know the Good Samaritan story. Malachi, we can have some coffee and talk about God…like you said one time?"

"What about your husband?" Malachi said. "Is he O.K. with ah…with me coming to your place?"

Right away, Malachi could see the tears in her eyes.

And then she said, "Do we have to stand here and blab about this stuff? Here? Here in the lobby of the county jail? Please, Malachi."

"O.K. …ah…," Malachi said. "Thank you, JC. I really appreciate your kindness. Ah…you kind of surprised me."

As they walked toward JC's car, Malachi said, "Your husband—he knows about this?"

"We don't live together anymore," JC said. "When he found out…" And then her eyes began to tear-up again.

Instantly, Malachi shook his head back and forth. His

mind fixed on her admission that flirting had caused her trouble. And he said, "That's why…that's why I wanted you to come to Jesus at Walmart, so you could get a new direction for your life…"

"You don't understand everything, Malachi," JC said. "I never thought this would happen…I mean…it's so hard to talk about it."

As they drove, conversation was sparse. Mostly the how's-the-weatherish variety. JC never said one word regarding Malachi's incarceration. Malachi was extremely tired from two nights of sketchy sleep, while JC seemed to be absorbed in her own thoughts.

He watched JC as she maneuvered through some morning traffic. He couldn't deny that he found her attractive.

She smiled a lot. Even as she was driving, Malachi noticed her pleasant expression.

And then Malachi focused even more attentively on JC but not on her appearance. He started rubbing above his right eye with his right hand. His face became warm on his right side, between his ear and eye—above his cheekbone.

And then it just came out of him, "Wow."

"What did you say, Malachi?"

"Do you remember when I told you that you were special in God's eyes?"

"I'll never forget it," she said as she glanced over at him.

Malachi pondered her response. Inside, he felt like he had in elementary school—when he saw a gold star on his report card.

"You never did answer me," JC said. "What did you say?"

"I said…ah." He paused, "JC, I'm just so tired. Could we continue this conversation after I get some rest? I'm exhausted."

"Sure. That'll be fine."

They drove on Highway 31, north out of Manistee and

then headed west on Coates Highway. At 8:42 in the morning, the sun was high enough in the sky to avoid windshield glare. The massive Manistee National Forest sprawled predominately to the south.

Fifteen minutes into the journey, JC turned left onto Archer Rd. and Malachi said, "My Uncle Dale lives out this way."

"Dale Marble?" JC said. "Sure, I've met him before. I don't know why I never made the connection."

"Maybe because we never use last names at Walmart."

"Yeah."

Malachi smiled when he saw that JC lived on a farm. He thought to himself, "A farm girl…a special one."

A dirt drive inclined upward, ending between the house on the left and a barn on the right. A towering hardwood stood between the two structures on the barn-side edge of the driveway.

The barn was mostly absent of paint—except for some hints of red. While the structure appeared sound, the exterior looked like a yearlong battle for a weekend warrior and his tools.

The house was a classic thirty-two foot by thirty-two foot square. A full-length columned porch extended across the front. A shed dormer protruding into the medium pitched roof formed a partial second story. The house, like the barn, was losing a few maintenance battles also.

JC pointed to the stairs. "Use the bedroom at the end of the hall. There's a bathroom up there. Make yourself at home. If you need anything, let me know. Otherwise, I won't bother you. But now, I need to get some sleep. I'm back at Walmart tonight at 10:00."

"Yeah," Malachi said as he thought to himself, "I wish I could say the same."

"Thanks for everything, JC."

"Thank you, God, for JC," were Malachi's final words before falling fast asleep in JC's guest bedroom.

10. New

Malachi laid in the bed, motionless. He had slept so soundly that it took him nearly a minute and a half to maneuver through: *who, what, when, where, why.*

It seemed by the hint of light coming in the window that the time was either at dusk or near sunrise. He didn't see a clock. But as the mental haze lifted, his mathematics deduced it was probably evening, and he had slept ten, eleven, maybe twelve hours.

A quick stop in the bathroom and he headed downstairs.

When he saw the clock on the kitchen wall, he said to himself, "That's unbelievable." It was 6:42 A.M. Then the thought popped into his head, "JC will be back from work in a half hour or so. Probably."

There was a note on the kitchen counter:

Malachi,

My home is your home. Food, whatever you need is yours. The laundry basket here in the kitchen has some clothes that might fit you. I hope you're here when I return from work.

JC

Though Malachi felt uneasy, he showered and ate a bowl of cereal. And just as he was nearly finished cleaning up, he heard a car making its way up the dirt driveway.

"This is very weird," he said to himself as he reflected on the strangeness of being in JC's home as he watched her walking toward the house.

"Good morning, JC," Malachi said. "I can leave anytime."

"You just got out of jail, your job is on the line, your car is in the Walmart parking lot, and you probably haven't even contacted anybody yet."

"Yeah, I'm still not fully awake. And my cell phone is at home. But I was concerned about you."

"You had breakfast?" JC said.

"Yeah."

"How about some coffee?"

Malachi smiled. "Uh, that sounds good. Really good."

As Malachi took his first sip, he said, "Do you know why I was in jail?"

JC laughed out loud. "I think everybody in Manistee knows why."

"Oh. Dumb question," Malachi said. "So, is everyone at Walmart talking about what happened?"

"No," JC said as she shook her head. "At the worker's team meeting the night after it happened, Sal came in and laid down the law. She announced that you had been arrested— but added no details. She was firm. She said she was going to stand by the Walmart policy that forbids work-related gossip or negative company talk. Of course, there are always the ones who still talk. Me? I like the policy. It makes the work place so much more…more peaceful."

"You're right about that," Malachi said. "Walmart knows what they're doing. That's why they're the best."

"So, everything was *peaceful*," JC said. "But Stu didn't show up and ah…when he misses work…it's usually…well, it's usually for a few days. And we know what that's about."

"It's sad," Malachi said. "I remember the first time I saw it happen…"

Stu was back the next night. He looked awful—pale, slumped shoulders, disoriented.

"It looks like someone beat you up," Malachi said.

"Someone did," Stu said. "The devil. And I helped him."

Malachi didn't ask what he meant. He knew.

Stu reminded him of Mel Fendman, an on-fire Christian like Stu.

Mel would stumble in his Christian walk—going off on partying binges. He was constantly up and down. When he was up, he was all about Jesus. And when he was down, it was sad. Pitiful. There were even times Malachi wondered if he would ever see him alive again.

"Yeah, I remember that time when Stu went off the deep end for a few days not long after you started working at Walmart," JC said.

"JC, if I tell you something, can you promise never to tell anyone?" Malachi said.

"Well…" JC wrinkled her forehead. "Well sure…I guess. I mean yes. Yeah, absolutely."

"Stu set me up out in the parking lot. He burned me."

"Yeah," JC said. "I figured it was something like that."

"You did?"

She nodded her head.

"Do you know why no one from the store came to your Jesus at Walmart meeting?" JC said. "You know, I was planning on coming."

"I thought we were talking about what happened in the parking lot. And now you're shifting gears on me. And you didn't even push in the clutch."

"No, it all ties together."

"What?"

"A few nights before the first meeting— it was your night off, Burt was in the store."

"He doesn't come to the store during third shift," Malachi said.

JC shook her head, "Yeah."

"So, what happened?"

"Now, remember Malachi, I didn't see everything," JC said. "But I do get around the store a lot with my job. So, I was making some observations."

"O.K. Sure. I understand," Malachi said.

"Red flag number one; Burt's at the store—at night. Then I noticed Stu was away from his aisle for…well, it was like an hour. And it wasn't break or lunch. And when I was making my rounds, I saw him leaving the office with Burt. They seemed particularly chummy. Face it—Stu is never actually chummy with anyone. Then, right away, Stu got on this crusade against Jesus at Walmart."

"What do you mean?" Malachi said.

"He snuck around convincing everyone that you were starting a cult."

"No."

"I'm telling you exactly what happened," said JC. "He was ferocious in his attack and just so zealous."

"So, how is Jesus at Walmart a cult? And me a cult leader?"

"You use the wrong version of the Bible—he hammered that one. And he would ask the question, 'So where did this mystery man come from? This mystery man who lives in a tent…deep out in the Manistee National Forest.'"

"So, where did I come from?"

"Let's see. How did Stu put it? O.K. here's what he said, 'From a lifestyle drenched in sin.' Then he would give us a spooky look and say, 'Is that someone you want to trust with your spiritual life…with your soul?' And then he would point his finger at us, 'Would you? Would you? Huh…would you?'"

"Wow."

"And then Stu linked you with that old guy…you know… people have seen you with him."

"Carl?"

"Yeah," JC said. "He is kind of freaky."

Malachi laughed. "Wow."

"There was more," JC said. "But…ah…we all…we just got apprehensive of you and Jesus at Walmart, actually fearful about it all."

"So, that's why, when the police were there, Stu said, 'He's involved in a cult and he planned on spreading the cult plague to Walmarts all over the country. Burt caught him.'"

"Exactly."

"And he totally believed it," Malachi said.

"Yeah. He sure did," JC said. "And everything he did was to protect us—his fellow workers."

"In a twisted way, Stu did it out of the goodness of his heart," Malachi said.

"I never thought of it that way."

"Very twisted," Malachi said.

He bowed his head, holding the cup with both hands. Like a beggar calculating how long before it would be empty, Malachi studied the half-inch of remaining coffee.

And then he raised his head back up in slow motion and

said, "And now, ladies and gentlemen, Malachi, the man of God puts the entire situation into the hands of God. With unwavering trust."

"That doesn't sound very convincing."

Malachi took a deep breath and exhaled. "JC, there's a cost to following Jesus. And right now...I'm feeling just about bankrupt. At the same time, this Bible verse keeps running through my head. 'The steps of a good man are established by the Lord and He delights in his way. When he falls, he will not be hurled headlong, because the Lord is the One who holds him with His hand.'"

Neither one said anything. JC watched Malachi.

He stared at the floor. And then looked at JC—but not in the eyes. "JC, I really want to believe that God is holding my hand. Because if He doesn't..." Malachi shrugged his shoulders.

"God will, Malachi."

Malachi smiled. "JC, you're special in God's eyes. Do you remember, while we were driving back from the jail, I told you we were going to talk about something at another time, after I got rested?"

"Yeah, I do."

"God showed me something about you," Malachi said. "First, you're pleasing Him. God is taking notice of the steps you have been taking to know Him. He sees you as you read your Bible, which is something new to you. I think God would say to you, JC, 'I'm worth the cost.'"

JC's lips began to quiver as she buried her face in her hands.

"You know, Carl, JC is a special lady," Malachi said.

"But she thinks I'm freaky," Carl said.

Malachi laughed.

"What so funny?" Carl said.

"I'm sorry," Malachi said with a smirk on his face.

"I've been called worse," Carl said.

"You know, when she drove me home, she told me that she and her husband—not really her husband—they never got married…well, he left her because she was reading the Bible and starting to talk about God. They had lots of other problems, but the God-thing caved in their already stormy relationship."

"She is special," Carl said.

"Wow. Even a freaky guy can tell," Malachi said.

II. Freesoil

"**M**alachi, you know, just sitting here in your Suburban…when you talk about what God's doing in JC's life and what happened when you met that guy in jail and those types of things, I start to sense the glory of God. Right now— as we're sitting here."

"But…"

"Exactly," Carl said as he pointed at Malachi.

"What do you mean?" Malachi said.

"In 2 Corinthians 3 it talks about our lives being transformed from glory to glory. One way I like to look at this is to see these glories as glorious things God is doing in and around our lives—and through us. Does that make sense to you?"

"Yeah…I think so."

"So in between these events—the glory to glory—is the to

time, the between times. For you, Malachi, it's like: God did this glorious thing—*but*. Then God did this glorious thing—*but*."

"So, you never do that, Carl?" Malachi said. "Waver during those gap times."

"Sure…but I always try to defy that type of mentality, that spirit," Carl said. "We follow Jesus. Our reaction to adversity needs to be radically different from those who don't know the Lord. A lot different—in every area of our lives. I mean…think about it; the Holy Spirit lives inside of us."

Malachi nodded.

"Remember when the Apostle Paul was stoned? The Bible says they thought he was dead. But he got up…and I'm sure he was hurting all over—big time," Carl said. "So, did he quit? Did the Apostle Paul leave the ministry? That would seem reasonable."

"No, he didn't," Malachi said. "I think it says he just went on preaching, probably the next day."

Carl could see Malachi's hands tensing up as he gripped the steering wheel.

He looked over at Carl. "But you know what happened to me after JC dropped me off at my place in Freesoil."

"Thank you, JC, for bringing me all the way down here to Freesoil," Malachi said. "Thank you for everything you've done for me. Everything."

"You're welcome, Malachi," JC said. "When did you move here?"

"On my last day off…I mean, I hardly have anything. So, it took like ten minutes to move. I never even told anybody yet. It happened so fast. And now I have to figure out where my Suburban is. Burt probably had it towed from the Walmart parking lot by now."

Malachi shook his head. "I have a lot of things I need to figure out."

Freesoil

And then he focused on JC. Her attention was on him also. They both looked like they were trying to summon the correct response at a spelling bee.

Malachi's lips tensed. Words eluded him as he thought in his mind, "What if I never see JC again?"

At that moment, JC grabbed Malachi and began sobbing. "What if I never see you again?"

With the *what if* remaining unanswered, Malachi waved as JC's car pulled out of the driveway.

Home was a simple house, a fourteen-year-old modular. Malachi's abode in Freesoil, located on the northern edge of town. And for this minuscule burg, it equaled being two blocks from Main St.—Freesoil Rd. A Dale Marble Construction sign was poked into the yard. Malachi's Uncle Dale had worked out a deal with the landlord, which included Malachi swapping some sweat equity for part of the rent.

Sparsely furnished would be an understatement. One over-stuffed chair with black corduroy-ish upholstery, while a card table and a single white plastic lawn chair comprised the balance of the furniture inventory.

On the card table, Malachi spotted his cell phone. He looked at it, imagining who would have left messages while he was gone. Carl, Pastor Jonathan, hopefully Mandy—"It would be nice to talk to her—and important."

The three messages from Sal were not expected. As Malachi tried to read her voice, the main thread seemed to be an ever-increasing intensity. Or was it anguish? Desperation?

Especially when the last one ended with, "Here's my cell phone number. Call me anytime. Anytime!"

Sal—one of Walmart's finest.

Malachi had nothing but respect for Sal. She would bark at you if she suspected you were slacking in the slightest. She had earned the right. The way Malachi saw it—she led by pure example. Her work ethic defined busting-your-behind.

Malachi didn't cherish the idea; it made his muscles sore the next day, but he was always willing to put it all on the line for Sal. He had never had a boss he respected more.

And Malachi knew, deep inside, she was soft as a marshmallow.

"Sal? This is Malachi Marble. You said it was O.K. to call your cell phone. Anytime."

"Oh Malachi…Malachi…"

"Sal, are you there?" Malachi said. "Sal?"

"How soon…so how soon can you…can you…" Sal said. "How soon can you meet me at the store, Malachi?"

Questions were flying through Malachi's head. But the tone of Sal's voice triggered a no-questions-asked urgency.

Except one. "What about Burt?" Malachi said. "I ah…"

"Burt won't be at the store," Sal said.

"You're sure. Right?"

"You have my word," Sal said. "So, when can you meet me at the store? How soon?"

"Whatever works for you, Sal."

"8:00 tonight?" Sal said. "I really need to get some sleep right now. I'm exhausted. Can you make it?"

"Yeah. Definitely. I'll be there," Malachi said. And then he thought to himself, "Somehow."

He held the cell phone in his right hand for a few seconds before placing it on the brown textured surface of the table. He noticed a hint of bottom-of-the clothes-hamper smell at his new residence as he stood in the silence. When he pondered his conversation with Sal, Malachi felt like an art patron standing before an abstract painting, asking, "What does this all mean?"

12. His End

Less than forty minutes later, Malachi heard a knock on his door.

"Mr. Malachi Marble."

"Yes."

"We have your vehicle."

"What's the deal?" Malachi said as he looked across the front yard and saw his Suburban on the flatbed of a red and silver tow truck.

"We're just here to drop off the vehicle," the man said. "That's all I know. And please don't ask me any questions. The boss said, 'Drop it off and don't say anything else.'"

"But ah…?"

"Where would you like the vehicle placed?"

"Along the edge of the street will be fine."

The man yelled, "You're good right there!"

And then he said, "Sign these papers, please, Mr. Marble."

Even before leaving Freesoil on his way to meet with Sal, he was trying to figure out what was going to happen. This train of thought had spent the day with him. Like a dog barking all night, it wouldn't go away. And it was irritating. Malachi wished he could shoot it—dead.

He had concluded for the twentieth time, as he neared the southern edge of Manistee, that Sal was going to terminate his employment. Sure, he might figure out a way to prove himself innocent of any crime. But plea bargaining, unfortunately, was a more likely scenario.

Then he said to himself, "I just want to get this over with."

Still one last thought nagged him, "Why isn't Burt doing the dirty work? What a coward."

As Malachi pulled into the parking lot, he pondered; what seemed like a month's time was actually less than four days.

He shook his head, "So much. Just so much has happened."

As he drove right to the spot where his life changed, he stared at the place in the parking lot where Stu had pinned him to the ground.

Malachi shivered as some pictures flashed through his mind. And then like a lick on the face from a cherished pet, a Bible verse surfaced in his mind. "For momentary, light affliction is producing for us an eternal weight of glory far beyond all comparison." This was one of the verses Carl had read to him a couple of hours before Stu slammed his body to the asphalt.

"Hmmm?" Malachi thought.

Malachi couldn't help it. He felt tingly all over. He had been praying, in some fashion, throughout the day. A central theme had emerged: "God bring me through. God, I trust You."

"Sal," he said as he knocked lightly on the office door,

which was three-quarters ajar. Sal sat peering at a computer screen. Even though Malachi could only see the side of her face through the open door, her looks startled him.

"Come…," Sal said; her face twitched. "Come in, Malachi, and ah…please close the door."

The moment Malachi released the door handle, tears started cascading down Sal's face.

Malachi froze, trying to grapple with his thoughts. "Should I hug her. What should I do?"

"Sal, what is it?" Malachi said as he reached both hands out toward her. She instantly clenched his hands and started to shake.

"He's gone," she cried.

"Who's gone?"

"Stu. He's gone," Sal said as she gripped Malachi's hands more intensely.

"Sal. Sal. It's not your fault they fired Stu," Malachi said. "What happened?"

"No." She stopped and took in a deep breath and then said, "Malachi…Stu…he…he took his own life."

"No!" Malachi said as tears flooded his eyes.

"What a shock. What a shock that was," Carl said. His right index finger brushed his lips before he continued. "So much has happened since then. It seems so long ago. I ah…I just don't know…I don't know…"

Malachi heard Carl sigh before he continued, "I still ponder it all…I just…I just thought…'Why God?'"

And then after several seconds of silence, he said, "I was already feeling the distress that night. When you called me before your meeting with Sal, I had to agree with your conclusion. When you called afterwards, I assumed it was to tell me you had lost your job."

Neither one spoke for several moments.

"Things still don't make sense to me," Carl said. "When Stu pinned you to the ground—thinking he was thwarting a cult, he must have felt like a hero. It's like a slugger hitting a homerun and then quitting the game after discovering he had run the bases the wrong way."

"It's my fault," Malachi said. "When I read the…when I read…when…"

Malachi shook his head. "I was just pretending. Pushing all that had happened into an out-of-the-way crevice in my brain. Now I know—it's my fault. I was just…"

"No, it's not your fault, Malachi. That's a lie from the devil."

"It is," Malachi said. "I knew something was wrong with Stu…I mean different than usual. Yeah, God didn't give me one of my *strong impressions or inklings*. But I knew."

"So, what were…?" Carl said.

"I was so busy with Jesus at Walmart. Getting things ready and all. I just ah…I just…" He rubbed his hair with his right hand as his focus shifted to the floor.

"No human can do everything," Carl said.

Malachi pounded his fist on the steering wheel. "I didn't want Stu to come to the meeting. I acted as if I did. I thought he would be disruptive—you know, questioning everything I said. It's like Jesus at Walmart is all about me. Why couldn't I trust God? Maybe make Jesus at Walmart all about Him—not me. If I couldn't hone the prickly edges off of Stu…I decided God couldn't either. I'm such a hypocrite. It's my fault Stu's dead."

Malachi opened the door and got out of the Suburban. He slammed the door closed and darted back to the spot where Carl first saw him. He scanned out over the endless expanse of the churning waters of Lake Michigan. His gaze then dropped down to the outcropping of rocks and stones three stories below.

His End

Carl caught up with Malachi and snatched him by the shoulders, spinning him around. "Stu made his own decision. What were you supposed to do?"

"Maybe I should have jumped."

"Quit it, Malachi. Now! Malachi, it's too late. Do something now. Honor Stu now. Honor God…now."

Carl held both of Malachi's shoulders firmly in his hands and said, "Look at me; God's mercies are new every morning." He hugged him. "Good morning, Malachi. God's mercies are new every morning. Good morning."

Malachi broke himself loose from Carl's embrace. "You don't understand."

At that moment, the intensity of Malachi's glare was like a blustery wind blowing up Carl's back.

Malachi spit his words out at Carl and walked away. "You didn't read the letter! You didn't read the letter!!"

13. The Letter

Malachi was putting the final touches on neatening the shelves in Department 13—Chemicals, when he heard overhead, "Malachi call 307. 307. Thank you."

It was the office. Sal's voice.

He picked up the nearest phone, kitty-corner from Chemicals in the Infants Department.

"This is Malachi."

"Sal here. Stop by the office before you leave work today. I have something for you."

"I'm pretty much done with zoning and everything else."

"Good. Come right now."

"Hmm?" Malachi thought, "I wonder what she wants," as he walked back to the office.

"Hey, come on in, Malachi," Sal said.

She turned back around, facing away from Malachi. Off to the right of the computer monitor, resting on a laminated countertop, she retrieved an envelope. Basic white. Legal size.

And then she turned around. "This came for you in the store's mail."

Malachi looked at it for a couple of seconds, and then Sal said, "I couldn't help noticing the return address. Is that Stu's father?"

"Yeah," Malachi said. His eyes slowly traced the name, Stewart Greyly Sr. and then he looked up at Sal. "Yeah…yeah that's Stu's dad."

Then they both stared at the letter in Malachi's hand. Both were silent.

Malachi drew in a deep breath. "Yeah. This is from Stu's father."

Like cutting a string to release a weight, Sal squeezed Malachi's left hand. "Hey Malachi, I never wished you a Happy New Year. Things got so busy tonight."

He looked at Sal's smile. "You're the best. God bless your New Year also, Sal."

Malachi walked slowly out to his Suburban, holding the envelope in his right hand.

The letter was a letter-in-a-letter. The first one had been written by Stu's father—Stewart Greyly Sr.

Dear Malachi Marble,

Doris and I want to thank you again for everything you did for us during the most challenging time of our lives. It seems like fate brought you into our lives at just the right time, and for that, we are very grateful.

I remember you told us that the grieving process is like a wound healing. It takes time. You told us that some wounds are deeper and that everyone heals at different rates.

As part of the healing process, Doris and I set a goal to be completely finished with cleaning out Stewart's place by the end of the year. We didn't hit the target. The wounds were too deep. We have done some things over there, but it's hard. Real hard.

The last time I was over there, I found this envelope for you. It was sticking out of Stewart's Bible. I had never looked in it. I'm not much of a Bible man. I had seen it before and just figured it was marking a place in the Good Book.

So here is the letter.

Thanks for everything,

Stewart

Malachi held the letter in his hand. He thought to himself, "This is like re-opening a grave."

Dear Malachi,

I knew you didn't want me involved in Jesus at Walmart. Who would?

I'm a drunk. I'm a drunk. I'm a drunk. Sure, I hide it almost all the time. But I remember the first time I came back to work after a binge. I could tell by the way you looked at me how evil you thought I was. When I said the devil attacked me, I'm sure you thought I was possessed. I'm sure everyone else at work thought the same thing. Maybe I am. Why would I act the way I do?

I'm such a hypocrite. I hate myself.

When I found out how that scumbag Burt had tricked me, I wanted to kill him. I knew it was that or have a few shots when I got home. Drinking is better than killing. Right?

That scumbag. Right after the police left, he said to me, "That will teach Malachi. He cannot mess with me. He is paying the price now. No one messes with me."

I said to him, "You said this whole deal was about saving the workers. It's about our Godly concern for the people we love. We're on a God-mission. What are you talking about now?"

We argued back and forth for quite a while. I knew then that it was nothing about you being a cult. And then when I said—well, I yelled it, "Just like the Bible says: 'Your sins will find you out.'"

That snake said to me, "You shut up, Stu, or you're next."

At home, I started looking through my Bible. Yeah, I've been drinking. I'm sure you can tell.

Here's what Psalm 44:13-19 says: "Thou makest us a reproach to our neighbours, a scorn and a derision to them that are round about us. Thou makest us a byword among the heathen, a shaking of the head among the people. My confusion is continually before me and the shame of my face hath covered me, for the voice of him that reproacheth and blasphemeth; by reason of the enemy and avenger. All this is come upon us; yet have we not forgotten Thee, neither have we dealt falsely in Thy covenant. Our heart is not turned back, neither have our steps declined from Thy way; Though Thou hast sore broken us in the place of jackals and covered us with the shadow of death."

God is speaking to me. The underlined words have revealed to me who I really am.

You know I'm not even sure what a jackal is. A coyote maybe. I wish I had one for a pet, a nice one that would lick my face.

Then Mister Malachi Marble—my best, best friend. My Jesus brother. Best, best friend. Forever. God showed me this verse.

I know it was God. I could hear His voice. His voice when I read this verse: "A good name is better than precious ointment; and the day of death than the day of one's birth."

Then I heard the voice say, "Stu, how good is your name?"

And then the voice said to me, "Stu the better thing. Stu the better thing."

Malachi, I only wish I could have helped you with Jesus at Walmart. I feel like crying. I remember exactly what you said not long before the first Jesus at Walmart meeting, "Stu, I was hoping you would want to get involved with Jesus at Walmart."

I remember. But what I remember more was the way that you looked at me. I knew you were thinking the exact opposite. The way you looked at me pushed me away...

Malachi's hands tensed so much on the letter that it crinkled under the tension.

Before reading anymore, he crammed the letter back into the envelope and sped out of the Walmart parking lot and drove to the park overlooking Lake Michigan, with the thought lodged in his brain, "It's my fault."

14. The Reading

Carl followed Malachi back to the Suburban and got in beside him. "Look at me, Malachi," he said. "So, the devil lies to Stu, and he believes it, and now you're joining in."

"You're twisting things," Malachi said.

"I'm twisting things?" Carl said. "Can I look at the letter?"

Malachi motioned his head toward the seat behind him. "It's back there."

Carl retrieved the letter and studied it for several minutes.

And then he said to Malachi, "You didn't read all of the letter?"

"No," he shook his head. "Not yet."

"You're falling for the basic method Satan uses. He always does. He always has. He always will," Carl said. "He baits us with partial truth. And when we cozy up to partial truth long enough, it appears to be pure truth. But it's not."

"Let's just break this letter down into some truth," Carl said. "O.K."

"Yeah. I guess. Sure."

"The rest of the letter gets even more garbled. I mean, even the parts you read didn't really make sense. Far from it. The way he...ah...the way he contorted the Bible verses. I mean, it's a shame. But bottom line—Stu was intoxicated. Right?"

"Yeah. Seems so."

"And some of these other verses he used are just...sad," Carl said as he furrowed his brow. "And he becomes almost incoherent when he wrote about all the broken relationships in his life. It seems like almost everyone in his life—it's so heartbreaking. And it sounds like he wasn't even going to church anymore. His ramblings are ah...really fuzzy—in just about every sentence."

"Well, I didn't read those parts," Malachi said.

"Except here. Did you read the last few sentences, Malachi?" Carl said. "Strange—Stu actually caught one last wave of clarity."

He handed the letter to Malachi and said, "Read the very last part of the letter."

Carl's finger touched the letter. "Read right here, Malachi."

> Malachi, can you do my funeral? I know I can trust you.
>
> I only have one request. Preach Jesus Christ and Him crucified. 1Corithians 2:2—"For I determined not to know anything among you, save Jesus Christ, and Him crucified."
>
> Malachi forgive me. God forgive me.
> Stu

"Still feel like jumping?" Carl said.

The Reading

Malachi closed his eyes. His left index finger and thumb lightly touched the outer boundaries of his eye sockets as his head slumped. A single tear trickled down his nose and moistened the letter.

"Oh Lord," Malachi said in a tone that sounded as if he was exhaling.

After several moments, Malachi raised his head and looked at Carl. "I wasn't going to jump."

With a hint of a smile on his face, Carl then drew in a breath before he said, "Look what God did, Malachi. Even though you didn't have the letter until months later, God made a way for you to honor Stu's request."

Malachi smiled, "Yeah…yeah. God is good."

15. How to Say Goodbye

Malachi sat in his new place of residence in Freesoil—located twelve miles southeast of the Walmart in Manistee. His laptop was open on the table as he prepared for Stu's funeral. His Bible—closed—rested beside it.

His wrenching, swirling emotions were thwarting his concentration. He still hadn't put all the pieces together why the duties had fallen to him.

And Stu's parents only brushed a few hurried strokes of information before Stu's mom closed the deal. "We don't have anyone else."

Malachi couldn't bring himself to ask about Stu's pastor. His mom already had tears trickling down her face. "Please."

Negotiations ended.

It did feel strange to be working out funeral arrangements

in a Walmart office. But Sal sliced a big chunk of the oddity off the plate when she gave Malachi the *look*. The just-like-a-mom look, "You'll do a wonderful job."

Malachi thought for a split-second she was going to add, "Son."

Instead, she hugged Stu's mom. "We loved your son so much around here. Everyone did." And then turned a gentle gaze toward his dad, "Everyone."

But now, Malachi was alone. The task loomed ahead of him. And adding to the challenge was the fact he had never officiated at a funeral.

"Oh crap." Malachi said under his breath. "I'm sorry, God…but this is too hard."

And then he heard a voice in his head. And it wasn't his own. "Is that what you would tell Mandy? What did you tell her about trusting Me and commitment?"

Instantly, Malachi recalled his words to Mandy, "God will give us the desires of our heart as we commit to Him and His ways and trust Him with all our heart. That He…God will do it. Am I making any sense to you, Mandy?"

Malachi's thoughts immediately started drifting. He made a feeble attempt to pry them in another direction, because at that moment, the funeral preparation and God were not in the spotlight.

Mandy. Yes, Mandy found her place at center stage. His mind flitted over the first phase of their relationship. They were drawn to each other the first time Malachi saw her at DT's—though it was subtle.

Her laugh captivated him. Not simply a laugh—she became the laugh. Her vocal inflection flowed out in a pleasing range of tone and volume as her face brightened like a flash bulb going off. Her body swaying gently. If *freedom* had a laugh, it would be Mandy's laugh.

How to Say Goodbye

Light flirting, some laughs, and even some serious issues poked their heads up as they built a relationship beyond the customer-waitress stage.

Mandy started joking about going out, while Malachi wondered why someone ten-years younger would want to date him. And then it happened with very little planning—their first date.

Malachi smiled as he remembered the two of them at the same overlook-park, where Carl and he were now parked. He lingered in the inner warmth as snapshots of their time together flowed through his mind.

And he still tingled as he recalled their final moments together that evening.

…Malachi walked Mandy to the door. He could feel his heart beating as she shifted towards him. They embraced.

So lightly.

So briefly.

Still, at that moment, Malachi knew he wanted to marry her. And he knew Mandy's thoughts toward him were the same.

Seconds later, as they said goodbye, feelings that deep remained properly concealed.

"Thanks for the great time, Mandy."

"Thank you, Malachi. See you soon."

And then Malachi bumped his thoughts back to the funeral. But then they flopped right back to Mandy. "I should call her."

"Hey Mandy," Malachi said.

"Malachi."

"You work today?" Malachi said.

"I'm going to DT's in about an hour and a half."

"Stu's parents asked me to officiate his funeral."

"What an honor," Mandy said. "You'll do great!"

"That's kind of what Sal said. Still, it's so difficult. I don't know…"

"Hold it, Malachi," Mandy said. "Aren't you the trust-God-guy?"

"Yeah," Malachi said. "God was just talking to me about that."

She laughed.

He smiled.

"Mandy, thanks for coming to Jesus at Walmart."

"You thanked me last time we talked."

"I know. But I was thinking again how amazing it was that you showed up, even after I told you I couldn't date you because…because…well, you know why."

"Yeah. It's ah…it's all going to work out…somehow," Mandy said. "So, when is the funeral, Malachi?"

"It's on Friday. 10:00 at Become Ministries."

"I'll try to make it."

"Well, back to work. Bye Mandy."

Once off the phone, Malachi prayed words from Psalm 19, "Let the words of my mouth and the meditation of my heart be acceptable in Your sight, O Lord—my Strength and my Redeemer." With that, his mind was primed and the thoughts started flowing readily.

He said to himself, "I need to call Sal if I'm going to do that."

"Hey Sal, this is Malachi. I hope you don't mind me calling your cell phone."

"No that's fine. Good to hear your voice," Sal said. "How are you doing?"

"I'm feeling…you know…emotions and grief…and responsibility all grabbing for a chunk of me."

"Yeah. I'm riding the same train," Sal said. "Speaking of responsibilities, I need to tell you something. Can we talk now?"

"Sure."

"Now Malachi, what I'm telling you is confidential."

"I understand."

"And off the record," Sal said. "I know I can trust you."

"You know you can, Sal."

"First, I want you to know that Burt is no longer with Walmart. Management will be informing the associates that Burt has been terminated—because he chose a direction in his life that was against company policy. But no more—end of story. So, what I'm telling you now is very sensitive. Very confidential. You understand?"

"Absolutely."

"Burt met his match," Sal said as she laughed. "He started putting pressure on me. And ah…"

"Flirting and way beyond," Malachi said.

"How did you know?"

"Um…ah. Sometimes, God shows me situations."

"So…what else do you know, Malachi?"

"There's nothing else…I mean…just tidbits…insights."

"Tidbits?"

"Sal, all I knew was that he was aiming at you…ah…I'll just say it…sexually. But that's it. Nothing else. I'm sorry I interrupted you. There's really nothing else."

"O.K. then," Sal said. "It's as you said, Malachi. You know, I never liked Burt anyway. And I have no tolerance for sexual advances at work. My dream is to be a Walmart store manager someday. Burt's flagrant disregard of strict Walmart policies could hurt not only this store and our employees, but he could jeopardize my career track as well. So, I decided to keep an eye on him. See what I could catch him in. It may sound harsh—but I wanted some revenge; it was payback time."

She paused for a few seconds and then continued, "When Burt came in the night of the first Jesus at Walmart meeting, I thought, 'What's going on here?' He doesn't come in on third shift. Never— except a week earlier, and that time, I saw him and Stu together. And when you were arrested, I wasn't buying it. I know you are a man of character and depth."

"Thank you, Sal."

"Maybe a little flaky sometimes," Sal said.

"O.K. let's just keep going with the story," Malachi said as he laughed.

"When they blamed you for disarming the parking lot cameras the night you were arrested, I instantly connected it with seeing Burt going into the security room during the same shift. Remember—I was keeping an eye on him," Sal said. "And I knew Seth was in the security room at the same time."

"I don't even know where the security room is."

"We keep it hush-hush. The cameras are on the stockers too—of course," Sal said. "Well the next night, after pondering your arrest and all the circumstances, I called Seth into the office. I didn't have any true evidence, but I decided to pull a bluff. I put on the *mean, snarly* Sal persona."

Malachi laughed.

"This Sal rarely makes an appearance," she said. "I blasted Seth the moment he closed the door. I yelled, 'I thought we could trust you. Last night, you went against everything Walmart stands for. Everything!' And then I turned off all my emotions like a light switch. I focused on his body language. Yep, I knew I had him. A few threats regarding jail time and Seth had a meltdown—and blurted out that Burt had bribed him. Seth admitted to disabling the parking lot cameras by manipulating a bogus computer system glitch."

Malachi shook his head. "Wow."

"There are a lot more details. Legal stuff and all that," Sal said. "But you know enough."

"Yeah. Thank you, Sal. Thank you so much."

"One more thing, Malachi," Sal said. "Walmart will treat

you right regarding all you've been through. I'll make sure of that."

"I have no doubt about it."

"So, why did you call?"

"This may sound like a strange request, but can I borrow Stu's pricing gun?"

"Stu's pricing gun?"

"Yeah," Malachi said. "It's for an illustration during his funeral."

"Sure," Sal said. "I'll leave it at the service desk. Pick it up anytime."

Malachi returned to his funeral preparations, feeling like an eighty-pound sack of potatoes had been cut loose from his back. As he typed away on his laptop, words flew from his fingers as ideas poured into his mind. His task had gone from a measure of dread to purposeful joy. He even found himself singing a song:

> Just Jesus, no strings attached
> Except the one that keeps pulling
> Pulling me back
>
> Back in the arms of Jesus today
> He took all my sins
> Sins away
>
> Away to heaven someday
> All my tears will be washed
> Washed away

Then the phone rang.

"Martin, this is a surprise."

"Hey Malachi, how are you doing?"

"You know, Martin, I'm grieving. And working on

funeral preparations—Stu's parents asked me to officiate the funeral—kind of seems over my head. But I was just singing."

"That's what I'm calling about."

"My singing?"

"No, my singing," Martin said. "Malachi, do you recall the first time we ever really talked? The first time we worked a full night together. I still remember what you asked me that night."

"So do I...

"So, what do you want to be when you grow up, Martin?"

"An ex-Walmart employee."

"Maybe you should aim a little higher."

"I just want to get out of here," Martin said.

"You must have a dream larger than leaving Walmart alive."

"Music's my thing."

Instantly, the door to Martin's dream opened as he confided in Malachi.

Martin played the guitar, bass, keyboard, mandolin, and sax. Guitar was his first choice. Seeing U2 in concert when he was a sophomore in high school initially inspired his dedication to music. He had devoured the guitar before branching out.

A member of several bands over the years, he had played in all the typical low-dough settings. A composer of dozens of songs, Martin had the majority of a CD recorded. The lack of time and money thwarted further progress.

"It's been a dry spot musically for me during the last year or so. My dream is shriveling...close to being dead...maybe forever."

"You need a wet spot, Martin," Malachi said. "It's like you're in the desert."

Martin looked around. "I'm definitely in a desert."

"Malachi, you said a bunch of other things that night—about God and life and other stuff," Martin said. "And I'll never forget that talk we had not long after you started working at Walmart."

"I never knew our conversation meant anything to you," Malachi said.

"Sometimes, a person needs time to process and work things out. Just on their own. If something starts to happen in a person—well, I guess it's like letting a plant do its own thing when it first breaks into the sunshine. If someone starts messing with it, poking at it all the time, he'll probably kill it. Just let the plant head toward the sun for a bit."

"Wow, Martin. Preach it."

Martin laughed.

Malachi didn't say anything. But in his heart, he was praising God—he had never heard Martin laugh before. Ever.

"I've hit a wet spot. And I have something I want to ask you," Martin said.

"Sure. Go ahead."

"I want to sing a song at Stu's funeral…and I ah…I want to sing it with JC."

"Wow you're full of surprises," Malachi said. "You and JC?"

"Yeah," Martin said. "We've been hanging out some. Here's another surprise for you—we've been talking about God and Jesus and stuff like that…and ah…it's been cool."

"But the night we worked together you told me you had a girlfriend and kids and you guys had been together for four years. Five years? What was it?"

"I lied," Martin said. "Yeah, there are a couple of kids. And I *had* a girlfriend. I lied though; she left almost two years ago. She came back three times—it didn't last long. But really, who would want to live with me—a Walmart stocker?"

"You can do a song, Martin," Malachi said. "You and JC. I'm really looking forward to it."

"What? I just told you I lied," Martin said. "Don't you think I'm a liar?"

"No, I ah…" Malachi said. "I think you're a little green plant heading toward the sun."

16. Goodbye Stu

The Lear 35 charter jet touched down at the Manistee County Blacker Airport located four minutes north of Manistee. It taxied down the west runway to complete its eight hundred and sixty-nine-mile journey from the south.

Two men in black suits adeptly made their way through the tiny terminal and drove south in their rental car. Like many people in Manistee and the surrounding area, they were making their way to Become Ministries—the church Malachi attended.

Management at the Walmart store had arranged to bring in help from the Walmart in Ludington, another beach-town twenty-nine miles away, so any associate who desired could attend the funeral for *Stewart Sheldon Greyly Jr.*

Malachi looked up when he had finished reading the

obituary.

He swallowed as his eyes scanned over the packed church. Fleeting thoughts of his own life-changing moments at the facility helped dial back his quivering emotions. He took a deep breath and felt a smile emerging as he thought, "This building is the perfect place for saying goodbye to a Walmart stocker."

The interior looked like a warehouse. The steel I-beam structure accentuated the industrial decor. Mega-rolls of insulation with a white plastic facing filled the wall's open cavities. The ceiling and walls with pipes, conduit, and miscellaneous mechanicals were painted an off-white. Generous overspray indicated a paint job executed by well-meaning volunteers.

The floor, which was basic gray, had many visible cracks. Malachi could imagine lift trucks darting about as he visualized the building's former life. A raw-wood stage held a fine selection of rock-band instruments. Two hundred chairs—blue economy models with entry-level padding, were set in neat semi-circular rows. A sound booth raised three feet above the concrete was perched in a rear corner. Behind the seating area, four rectangle tables lined up parallel near a large bank of shelved books.

"I would like to thank everyone for coming today. As family, friends, and coworkers, we have gathered today to say goodbye to Stu. If you are not, my hope is that you too, by the end of the service today, will be able to say you are an admirer of Stu. Not because he was perfect, but because of some of the beautiful things he did during his life. And even in the midst of his struggles, Stu so desperately wanted to share something with each one of us."

Malachi stepped away from the podium and paced toward the center of the platform, holding a notebook in his right hand. "As a tribute and a way to show our admiration for Stu, if he touched your life through his sacrificial kindness, could you please raise your hand?"

Malachi swallowed hard as he fought back tears. There were more hands than he could readily count.

"Mr. and Mrs. Greyly," Malachi said as he extended his hand toward them, "please look around and see some of your son's admirers."

Moments after they turned to look, Stu's mother began to sob. His father lowered his head as he put his arm around his wife's shoulder.

Malachi rubbed his left hand over his lips and took a deep breath. "On third shift, Stu was known as *The Finisher*. How many third shifters here today are glad for The Finisher?"

Malachi raised his hand, along with many other hands, while a few hardy vocal responses sounded.

"For all of you who sleep during the night and aren't exactly sure how all the merchandise gets on the shelves at Walmart, I'm here to tell you it's hard work. Real hard work. And sometimes, we overnighters wonder how we're going to complete our tasks. Sometimes, the situation seems impossible. Then Stu, The Finisher, would arrive and bail us out. He didn't ask for anything. No payment. Mr. Super Stocker would just show up and rescue us."

By now, Malachi was striding, bouncing back and forth along the stage. "And I don't know if I ever really thanked Stu enough."

He raised his left hand. "How about you? Let's give it up for The Finisher."

Celebration instantly reverberated throughout the building.

Malachi power punched the air, "Yeah!"

He then slowly walked back and forth, looking over those who had gathered.

He glanced at the notebook in his right hand and then toward the audience. "Two Bible verses come to mind when

I think of The Finisher. And with a great deal of sorrow, we need to accept the harsh fact that Stu...Stu didn't finish his complete course."

Malachi shifted his eyes upward for a second. "But it's like in a race, say a relay race, when a teammate drops the baton during a handoff; we pick up the baton. We carry on."

He extended his hand toward the audience. "I'm asking each one of you to honor what Stu meant to you by carrying on some of his ideals. Ideals that The Finisher...did not finish."

He moved to the center of the platform. "Friends, today I'm asking you to pick up the baton. Finish your race. Honor Stu."

Once again, he looked at his notes. "In Jeremiah 29:11 it says, 'For I know the plans I have for you, declares the Lord. Plans to prosper you and not harm you. Plans to give you hope and a future.'"

He looked up. "For each one of us, no one is excluded. God has good plans for our lives. For most of us, this likely means we have not arrived at that place, the place where God wants us to find, to experience, to flourish in what He desires our lives to be."

Malachi raised his hand in the air. "I'm not there. But I know for sure—I'm heading there. For many here today, a career at Walmart is not God's ultimate plan for your life. In this room today, there are future teachers, pastors, administrators, builders, stay at home moms, and more, who need to get on track so they can finish what God desires for their lives."

He slowly panned the audience with his eyes. "In the Bible it says, 'Let us fix our eyes on Jesus, the author and finisher of our faith. Who for the joy set before Him endured the cross, scorning its shame, and sat down at the right hand of the throne of God.'"

"Here we encounter the ultimate finisher—Jesus Christ. Here's the deal: if you want God's prosperous life to flow in your life, you need Jesus Christ in your life."

Malachi tilted his head, looking upward for several seconds and then returned his attention to the audience. "Almost everyone here knows what I'm talking about. The message of the cross of Jesus, the Good News, the Gospel, is well-known in this country. It's everywhere. Can anyone miss it? Can anyone avoid it? Jesus hung on the cross. Beaten. Bleeding. Humiliated. On the cross He said, 'It is finished.'"

He walked over to the podium, placed his notepad on it, and reached underneath and pulled out Stu's pricing gun. He lifted it above his head. "Anyone know how to work one of these?"

Malachi turned the dial to set a price and slapped a price sticker on his suit coat near his left bicep. "It says $5.55."

Malachi almost laughed when he heard someone yell, "Sold."

He then dialed in a new price and affixed another sticker to his jacket. "It says $5,555.00. Any takers?"

He set the pricing gun down and then looked around. His fingers interlocked as he stood peering over the sanctuary. "The cost. The cost is too high."

Malachi stood silent for several seconds and then held out his hands—palms up. "Today, Jesus holds out His nail scarred hands and says, 'It is finished.' Father God looks at each one of you with love and promises, 'I have plans to prosper you. Not to harm you.' And then too many people focus on themselves and say, 'The cost—it's too much. I can't.'"

Malachi scanned over the audience. His facial expression looked like a man who was looking for a trail through a grove of trees. But in his mind, he was asking, "What next, God?"

Malachi then motioned to Martin and JC. "Two of our Walmart overnighters want to do a song to honor Stu. And then I'll have a few closing comments."

He extended his hand toward them. "Thank you, Martin and JC." And stepped down from the platform.

"Hey everybody," Martin said. "JC and I sort of looked around the God-world of music and found this song. In one of the parts of the Bible...one of the books...I think it was Roamers."

He glanced over at JC as she quietly said, "Romans."

"In Romans," Martin said, "we found where it said, 'All have sinned and fallen short of the glory of God.'"

He strummed his guitar lightly as he continued to speak, "I've...I'm coming to the conclusion that pretending I'm something I'm not doesn't make any sense. Come on, we're all....it's ah... like the Bible says, 'All have sinned.'"

Martin shifted his eyes downward.

After a couple of moments, he looked back up and measured out his words, "This song is for me. This song is for you." He pointed his finger upward. "This song is for you Stu. This song is for you, my dear friend."

> Softly and tenderly Jesus is calling
> Calling for you and for me
> See, on the portals He's waiting and watching
> Watching for you and for me
>
> Come home, come home
> You who are weary, come home
> Earnestly, tenderly, Jesus is calling
> Calling, O sinner, come home
>
> Why should we tarry when Jesus is pleading
> Pleading for you and for me
> Why should we linger and heed not His mercies
> Mercies for you and for me

Goodbye Stu

Come home, come home
You who are weary, come home
Earnestly, tenderly, Jesus is calling
Calling, O sinner, come home

Time is now fleeting, the moments are passing
Passing from you and from me
Shadows are gathering, deathbeds are coming
Coming for you and for me

Come home, come home
You who are weary, come home
Earnestly, tenderly, Jesus is calling
Calling, O sinner, come home

Oh, for the wonderful love He has promised
Promised for you and for me
Though we have sinned, He has mercy and
pardon
Pardon for you and for me

Come home, come home
You who are weary, come home
Earnestly, tenderly, Jesus is calling
Calling, O Stu, come home

O Stu, come home

Malachi struggled to regain his composure. His eyes
were teary. A few tears trickled down his face, and he could
hear sobbing all around.

Finally, he made his way back upon the stage. He stood
there as another wave of emotions gripped him.

And then, after several more seconds, he looked over at Martin and JC, who were now sitting on the front row. "Thank you. Wow, that was awesome."

His focus then returned to those gathered. "In closing, honor Stu—pick up the baton for him. Be a finisher. In your work life. In your faith life. Pay the cost. Jesus did."

He pointed back to the sound booth. "Pastor Jonathan, the pastor of this fine church, is always ready to tell anyone about making a connection with the ultimate Finisher—Jesus Christ. He's back there in the sound booth. I'm available. Every Thursday in the middle of the night, during third shift lunch hour, I'm leading a meeting called Jesus at Walmart. Anyone can attend."

With those words, an invitation to a fellowship luncheon, and a prayer, Malachi dismissed everyone.

"Pastor Marble," Malachi heard as the attendees began to disperse.

He turned. Two men in black suits were standing to his right. The taller one said, "That was an exceptional service, Pastor Marble."

"Thank you," he said. "Please call me Malachi."

"I hear you're one of our associates."

"Yes sir, I am."

"Call me Mike."

"Thank you, Mike. Praise God for your encouragement."

"I do have one concern," Mike said as he smiled. "Were you trying to convince everyone to quit working at Walmart?"

They both laughed.

"God's will, Mike. God's will."

He looked Malachi directly in the eye and extended his hand. The feel was especially firm as Mike said, "God's will, Malachi."

17. The Kind of...Revival

"**Y**ou know what, Malachi?" Carl said as he leaned forward in the Suburban's seat. "That was one of the finer funerals I've been to in my life. I've been to a lot of them. And Martin and JC—they were amazing. The song they picked was so perfect.'"

"I told you; I know I did," Malachi said. "I had no idea what song they were going to sing."

"See Malachi, when something like that happens, you know God's hand is upon it."

"Definitely."

"I felt poked...you know, by the Holy Spirit, by your words," Carl said.

Malachi looked over at Carl. "I never told you, but when I went home, some of my own words poked me."

"I've experienced that myself."

"But I also felt a lot of conviction," Malachi said. "I was really feeling the grip on my soul. And then I plopped my Bible open and my eyes fell on a couple of verses, "'Who may ascend into the hill of the Lord? And who may stand in His holy place? He who has clean hands and a pure heart…'"

Malachi shifted in his seat and looked away from Carl. "Several people offered accolades after the funeral, like that guy in the black suit—the one dressed so nicely."

"Who was that?" Carl said. "I noticed him."

"I had never met him before. His name was Mike," Malachi said. "Very sincere and complimentary. But when I got home, I was feeling, 'Wow. I really did a great job. Wow. Malachi, you were amazing.'"

Malachi shook his head. "Pride had entered my heart. And then I'm thinking to myself, 'How am I going to experience God's prosperous life if I don't acknowledge Jesus as the author and finisher of the things He does in my life?'"

"And then what usually happens is that we swing the pendulum to the opposite spectrum," Carl said. "And we totally lack any self-worth."

"Exactly," Malachi said. "How did you know?"

"It's a common tactic of the enemy," Carl said. "He'll kick one leg out from under us by pointing at our pride and then kick the other one out by convincing us that we're worthless. And bam, we fall on our face, usually having a little pity party."

"That's exactly what happened at the next Jesus at Walmart meeting," Malachi said. "The funeral was on Friday and then the next Thursday during third shift's lunch hour, I'm heading to the conference room thinking, 'God, why do I always feel so inadequate?'"

"Realistically, it didn't make any sense at all that you were feeling that way. Did it, Malachi?"

"No, not at all."

"But then…"

"Yeah, I still remember…"

Carl came up to Malachi at that moment and said, "Don't forget what the Bible says about the Apostle Paul, 'I was with you in weakness and in fear and in much trembling. And my message and my preaching were not in persuasive words of wisdom. But in demonstration of the Spirit and of power, so that your faith would not rest on the wisdom of men, but on the power of God.'"

And then Carl touched his shoulder. "Malachi, it's time to demonstrate His power."

At least half of the stockers were present.

Even Sal. Which prompted Malachi to recall the time he had asked her, "Do you ever go to church?" She had responded, "Let's talk about that another time."

As he looked around the room, he saw a few faces he didn't recognize. And with only an hour, there was no time for meet and greet.

There was Gary. Second row left. Malachi thought about the time they were on the verge of a shoving match over who owned a pallet jack—the one Malachi had been using. Malachi smiled when he remembered how his apology had led to a brief conversation regarding Gary's church attendance habits.

"Praise God," Malachi said to himself.

In the back row—on the end—it was Erin and Gret.

Malachi remembered when he first invited them.

It was a pleasant mental picture: "You probably don't want us at your meeting," Erin had said after Malachi had invited them.

"Why's that?" Malachi had replied.

"We're gay."

"So?"

"You must think we're…sinners."

"I'm not going to pretend I agree with you…about what you're doing or understand what you're doing," Malachi said. "You know what…I can't even figure out why I do some of the stuff I do."

Malachi paused. And heard words in his head, "Follow the way of love."

"Is it just me," Malachi said, "or is it hard to be a human sometimes?"

Erin and Gret said, "Yeah," in perfect unison.

All three of them chuckled.

"Here's the deal," Malachi said. "Jesus at Walmart isn't about me figuring out all the stuff everybody's doing wrong. Jesus said, 'I came that they may have life and have it more abundantly.' There's no dash, dash: except Erin and Gret, at the end of that verse. And if you look on the flyer, you won't find a list of excluded people. I want you two to come."

"Thanks," Erin said. She glanced at Gret. "We just might drop by."

Malachi squeezed Mandy's hand gently before going to the front of the group and said softly to her, "Thanks for coming."

His eyes surveyed the group gathered. It seemed like their faces were as sad as they had been at the funeral.

As Malachi tried to string his thoughts together regarding the words he had prepared for the meeting, it was like trying to play a song on a horrendously out of tune guitar—missing a string.

He just could not press the inner discord from his spirit.

With hesitation he said, "Hey everyone, let's get started—welcome to Jesus at Walmart."

Malachi sat down facing those gathered. He flipped through his Bible and then said, "Let's pray before we start."

Everyone bowed their heads.

"Father God in your Word, your Bible, the Apostle Paul

said, 'I was with you in weakness and in fear and in much trembling.' Dear God, I acknowledge before these gathered and You that tonight I am here before them in the same way. Dear Father God, we need your message tonight. We need preaching from You. I acknowledge also that I have no persuasive words of wisdom to offer the people sitting in front of me. Dear God, I thought I did. Please I need…we need a demonstration of the Spirit and of power, so that our faith will not rest on the power of Malachi Marble, but on Your power God. Ah..."

Malachi tried to say something, but it was as if he couldn't speak. His eyes were still closed as he sat there in the long silence. A peace ascended into the room. No one seemed antsy. The silence felt restful. God-inspired. Two, three, four minutes.

And then he heard the sound of crying moving towards him. He opened his eyes and kneeling right in front of him was JC. "I want to get saved right now. I want Jesus."

So, Malachi knelt down beside JC and put his arm around her shoulder. And as he was about to say something to her, he heard a voice above him.

"Me too." It was Martin. "I'll pay the cost to follow Jesus." And then he joined them on the floor.

Malachi talked and prayed quietly with them as they huddled on the floor. At one point, all three of them were weeping. And then like an awareness of a distant radio sound, Malachi's mind and ears briefly relived a few moments of Stu's funeral…

>Softly and tenderly, Jesus is calling
>Calling for you and for me
>See, on the portals He's waiting and watching
>Watching for you and for me

Come home, come home
You who are weary, come home
Earnestly, tenderly, Jesus is calling
Calling, O sinner, come home

When they arose from the floor, Malachi sucked in deeply to keep the tears from flowing.

JC and Martin faced Malachi as if they were awaiting further instructions.

Malachi glanced at Mandy. She looked away. He could see tears in Sal's eyes. And Gary had his head bowed—and seemed to be praying.

Malachi thought quickly to himself, "What should I do now?" as the solemn group stared at him. And so were JC and Martin.

Instantly, an idea popped into his head. He turned JC and Martin around like a newly married couple. "Ladies and Gentlemen, I would like to introduce to you JC and Martin—two brand new followers of Jesus Christ."

Everyone cheered—as if they were exhaling all their silenced emotions.

"You may now kiss Jesus Christ, your new Savior," Malachi said.

JC laughed and blew a kiss heavenward.

And then Martin did the same thing. They embraced each other as they giggled like children.

18. To You O Lord I Lift Up My Soul

"**T**o You O Lord, I lift up my soul," Malachi said in a whisper as he stared out the windshield.

"What did you say, Malachi?" Carl said.

"To You O Lord, I lift up my soul," he said. "That meeting, back all those months ago, was so awesome…one of the best memories of my life. But why do things have to fizzle so quickly. It's ah…O my soul."

He quickly looked over at Carl. "Don't give me that, 'You planted seeds blah, blah.' And if I hear, 'It's God's timing,' one more time, I might puke. Oh, I know, this one really sounds holy, 'It is…the Holy Spirit's work…you do your…part…let God...be God!'"

"You better watch it, Malachi. God might give you leprosy of the mouth."

"To You O Lord, I lift up my soul," Malachi said again. "Carl, sometimes I wonder, 'Why can't things ever work out for me?'"

Malachi, the Bible says, "'The time will come when people will not listen to sound doctrine, but will follow their own desires and will collect for themselves more and more teachers who will tell them what they are itching to hear. They will turn away from listening to the truth and give their attention to legends.' Bottom line—it's becoming tougher and tougher to keep people connected and committed to Jesus Christ. It's one of the things you emphasized at Stu's funeral—the cost. I mean...face it, just about everybody wants it easy."

"For me, I'm not looking for...I mean...easy," Malachi said. "But when the group dwindles from two dozen to a dozen and then to half a dozen in three weeks, I'm thinking, 'What am I doing wrong?' Maybe I should have had some snacks or something."

"Like hot dogs?" Carl said.

"Hot dogs? What do you mean...I was thinking *snacks*. You know..."

"A wise pastor once told me, 'If you have to use hot dogs to get them to attend, you'll have to keep feeding them hot dogs to get them to stay,'" Carl said. "Malachi, you need to do what the Bible says. Listen to this verse and let it sink in, 'But you must keep control of yourself in all circumstances. Endure suffering, do the work of a preacher of the Good News and perform your whole duty as a servant of God.'"

"Oh great, endure suffering," Malachi said.

"The cost," Carl said as he looked over at Malachi.

"Yeah I know...but there was this one night...it was like three weeks after the *big* Jesus at Walmart *kind-of-revival*."

"How's everyone doing tonight?" Sal said. "Hey gang, it looks like, for the most part, it's going to be an easy night.

And we all like easy around here."

Malachi looked around the break room as the third shift stockers were receiving their instructions before heading out to their assigned aisles and departments.

He saw many smiles when their shift manager said, "Easy." Additionally, some affirming hoots sounded.

Sal continued, "Now, a couple of departments have their normal amounts of freight, and Frozen is even a touch on the heavy side. My goal tonight is to have all the freight on the shelves by second break—that includes zoning. So, let's do a really top-notch job on zoning. Let's make those shelves look their best. And then during the last two hours, I have some special projects. You know—like cleaning under the shelving units."

Malachi agreed when he heard someone say, "Yuck."

After everyone was assigned their duties, a quick round of mandatory stretches followed, and then a semi-hardy, "One, Two, Three Walmart," before the stockers found their purposeful stride.

Malachi's regular Department—Chemicals, had the normal amount of skids stacked high with bleach, soap, mops, laundry products, and the like. So, Sal assigned Erin to work with Malachi.

"Erin, have you ever worked Chemicals?" Malachi said as he lowered the last skid to the floor.

"Yeah…once at the end of a shift when you weren't here," she said.

"So, you kind of know where things go?"

"Kind of," Erin said. "Hey Malachi, I ah…we were going to talk to you. Gret and me."

"What about?"

"Well, we stopped coming to Jesus at Walmart. And ah…"

"Yeah, I was wondering what happened."

"We're going to church now," Erin said, "almost every

Sunday."

"Wow," Malachi smiled. "Praise God."

"We're really getting into it."

"So, where are you attending?"

"It's a new church—Lakeview Extended Grace."

"Lakeview Extended Grace?"

"Yeah. We love it. They accept Gret and me just as we are. No one is judgmental. They are so open-minded. They're on the cutting edge in so many ways."

"What do you mean?"

"I mean, they understand how God made Gret and me. At Lakeview Extended Grace, they also reach out to those rejected, neglected, and pushed away by regular churches by embracing cannabis Christians."

"Cannabis Christians?" Malachi said. "What's that about?"

"It's all about compassion. Lakeview Extended Grace wraps its loving arms around those who need medical marijuana to combat their suffering. Compassion...you know—the compassion of Jesus."

Malachi wanted to interrupt, but Erin's word flow was on speed dial.

"We've been studying a book about *love*," Erin said. "It's an awesome book. It has caused me to conclude that there is no hell. And that love will triumph in the end."

And then she looked intently at Malachi. "Oh Malachi—what a freeing thought. I feel so free. Have you heard of the book?"

"No hell?" Malachi said. "Yeah. It rings a bell."

Malachi concentrated on Erin's facial expressions for several seconds and then said, "Erin...ah...have you...you and Gret checked all this stuff out...I mean...checked it out in the Bible?"

She instantly scrunched her face. "Malachi...Malachi,

come out of the darkness and fear and ignorance and enter into the healing light of the Gospel of Jesus."

Malachi mumbled under his breath, "The Gospel of Jesus Christ."

"What?" Erin said.

"Ah…hey…ah we've got shelves to stock," Malachi said.

"Hey Sal, where do you want me to go next? Erin and I've knocked out Chemicals."

"The zoning is all done?" Sal said.

"It looks beautiful."

"Go help Gary in frozen," Sal said. "He actually got a big load tonight—a bunch of ice cream."

"Sal, you got a few seconds to talk?"

"Sure."

"Let's see," Malachi said. "Ah…I was wondering…I mean, concerned…I was curious—why I haven't seen you at Jesus at Walmart?"

"Because I'm not there," she said as she smiled.

"Wow. That's profound," Malachi said. "No really, really Sal."

"I'm so busy. Often, I'm working on things during lunch."

"Too busy for…for a little God-time."

"Malachi, I'm happy for you. I see your focus on God. And there is something intriguing about it all. But…I don't know." She paused as her eyes turned away.

And then she refocused on Malachi. "You're a stocker. A good one. A really good one. But the reality…your responsibilities are limited. It's a job to you. Walmart is a career for me. I want to be the best I can be. And there's a price to pay when you aim toward the top. My goal is to manage a store someday. I don't want to be an assistant manager—a third shift one no less. Believe me, Malachi, I've weighed things out. Attending Jesus at Walmart or shifting my focus to God-time…"

She paused and shook her head before continuing, "I have

to make a choice. What's better for me? What's better for my career?"

"But…"

Sal raised her hand with the palm facing Malachi. "I have a lot of respect for you, but it's not for me."

She grinned unnaturally. "Your few seconds are up." She pointed. "Frozen—go help Gary."

"Hey Gary, what do you want me to do?"

"There's one more skid of ice cream back in the freezer. It's a small one. Go get it."

"You got it."

"If you can knock that out, I'll get everything else," Gary said. "And don't forget ice cream melts, so you've got to blast through it."

"Ice cream melts?" Malachi said. "I recall you saying that the time you stole my pallet jack."

"Your pallet jack? Your pallet jack?" Gary said. "I think Walmart owns all of the jacks."

Gary laughed.

"Yeah, I was about to punch you…over a stupid pallet jack."

Gary laughed again, "But we kissed and made up."

"And right after I apologized, I asked you about church, and a week later, I invited you to the first Jesus at Walmart."

"Yeah, I kind of remember."

"And then you came that one time. It seemed like God touched you…maybe?"

"Yeah, I felt God that night…definitely," Gary said. "But then over the next week or so—when I started thinking about some of the things you were saying, it just didn't hit my ears the right way."

"What do you mean?"

"I used to go to church. And I was always taught that Jesus—having Him in your heart was free. But you kept talking about *the cost*. It just didn't hit my ears right."

"Gary, Jesus is free. But if you want to be a true follower of His, there is a cost."

"That's not exactly what I've heard. Jesus came to bless me."

"I think dying on a cross for a sinful human is a blessing," Malachi said.

"No, you don't get it, Malachi. I mean—what about a nice car? A nice house? Blessings from Jesus—that's the Jesus I want to follow."

"The no-cost Jesus," Malachi said. "You want to be free. Free to be uncommitted to church attendance. Free not to serve the Lord Jesus. Free not to live a holy lifestyle. Oops—did I say, *holy-lifestyle* in public? Just no cost. Free to…"

"How about free not to listen to you?" Gary said as he turned and walked away.

Malachi looked at Carl. "O.K. I could have handled that one better."

"Definitely," Carl said. "But it does sound like a rough night."

Then Carl continued, "Praise God; JC and Martin are steady Jesus at Walmart attendees. God is working in their lives. I can see it. Can you?"

"Yeah, of course," Malachi said. "But that first meeting after the funeral, there must have been close to twenty-five people. And now—only a handful show up."

They both sat quietly for a few moments before Malachi said, "I wish I didn't think this way. But I do. I keep wondering when will Martin and JC drop out."

"Why would you think that way, Malachi?" Carl said. "You can see the changes in their lives. Godly changes. It's remarkable. It's truly remarkable."

"Carl…I just can't help it. I mean…"

Malachi took a deep breath and sat there staring out the windshield.

And then after nearly a minute of silence, he said, "Those thoughts are often triggered when I think back…when I start thinking back about the Mandy thing."

19. The Mandy Thing

She seemed to be the only bright spot in Malachi's life during the darkest point of his life. And if not the only one, Mandy Howard was by far the brightest. A waitress at DT's Good Time Place—a well-established eating and drinking spot in downtown Manistee.

The day Malachi met Mandy, he felt like a shipwreck survivor who had washed up on shore. And that shore was the small city of Manistee, Michigan, located halfway between Chicago and the northern tip of Michigan's Lower Peninsula on the shores of Lake Michigan.

Only eight hours before he met Mandy, Malachi was a resident of St. Amos—seven hours southeast, near Michigan's southern border.

Malachi had chosen Manistee because his Uncle Dale

Marble had a construction company that serviced the area. And he once told Malachi there was always a construction job waiting for him. Malachi surprised Uncle Dale by arriving un-announced.

Uncle Dale had his own surprises. Some poor business decisions, an abrupt downturn in the economy, and too many visits to the casino north of town had left him bumping up against bankruptcy. And beyond all that, he was fighting a battle with cancer.

Malachi discovered all this the day he had escaped from St. Amos. Their conversation took place at DT's. And Mandy had waited their table.

Malachi still laughs to himself when he thinks about the time Mandy playfully accused him of flirting.

As Mandy poured the coffee that day, Malachi had noticed her fingers. They were long. Thin. Elegant.

Malachi felt stupid the second the words left his mouth; they tumbled out without any effort or thinking. "You have beautiful fingers."

Mandy laughed out loud. And Malachi's face approached the same rust-red color as her shirt.

"I've never heard that pick-up line before," she said.

"I'm sorry," Malachi said as his eyes retreated toward the coffee cup in his hand. "I meant...I mean. I...well you do have beautiful fingers. And...I was just thinking how they looked perfect for playing guitar. That's all I meant."

"You're different. Aren't you? I mean in a good way," she said.

From then on, it seemed to Malachi that Mandy became the flirty one. And after he told her about his new job at Walmart, she said, "So when are we going to go out and celebrate?"

Not long after that, they did.

While issues arose after that delightful time together,

Malachi was now feeling secure in what he considered a growing relationship.

Or was it?

Malachi tried to press it out of his mind, but the thoughts kept pressing back, "Is Mandy acting different? Is she trying to pin me down to exactly when I'm going to show up at DT's? Is something going on? Am I imagining things?"

A month plus a few days had passed since the questioning initially entered his mind. Malachi was shoving liquid detergent bottles onto the shelves—it was around 2:00 A.M, when he heard someone screaming, "Malachi! Malachi!"

The sound was so pleading that a spike of fear pulsed through his body as his head jerked toward the voice.

It was Alex, Mandy's son who had just turned eleven. He was sprinting toward Malachi.

Because he was breathing so hard, it was all he could do to blurt out, "He's hurting Mom. Kenny's hurting Mom. He's hitting my mom."

As they dashed for the door, Malachi saw JC and hollered at her, "Tell Sal I have to leave. It's an emergency."

Malachi's Suburban had never accelerated this fast as they bolted from the parking lot. On the way, Malachi said to Alex, "Why didn't you get the neighbors?"

"They're already afraid of Kenny," Alex said.

In less than two minutes, they were there, on 12th St., about fifteen blocks north of downtown and less than a half-mile from Walmart. In a tree-lined residential area, Mandy lived in the upper unit of an old white two-story house converted into two apartments.

When Malachi arrived at the closed door with Alex directly behind him, he stopped and listened to appraise the situation.

The yelling on the other side was loud, vulgar, and significantly incoherent.

Malachi turned around and looked directly at Alex. "Don't believe what he's saying about your mom."

Alex nodded his head.

"You stay out here. O.K."

Alex nodded his head again.

"Help me, God," Malachi said to himself. Then he turned the knob and stepped in.

He instantly caught a big whiff of marijuana smoke. Even while outside he thought he had smelled it. A bottle of whiskey and a bottle of tequila were on the dining room table. Both were the type that arrive in plastic bottles. The tequila container was on its side—appearing to be empty. Beer cans in two different colors found homes in a variety of locations. A couple of them no longer had their original shape.

Malachi was certain the baggie on the end table was weed. Rolling papers rested nearby.

One of the curtains hanging over the window facing the street had been wrenched enough to cause a three-inch droop in the center of the curtain rod. And two of the three sofa cushions were on the floor.

Even the adrenalin rapidly coursing through his veins couldn't subdue the terror he felt when Kenny's eyes met his.

Still, Malachi drew first and bellowed, "What are you doing?"

As Kenny steadied his swaying, he stared intently at Malachi, glared at Mandy, and then looked back at Malachi. "Whatever I want, preacher boy."

"Not while I'm here. And I'm here to stay," Malachi said.

Then he heard Mandy shriek, "What are you doing here, Malachi!"

Suddenly, he felt nauseated when he saw her struggling to keep her balance. Mandy's blouse was unbuttoned a button too low—maybe two, while her hair looked like it had encountered a multi-gust barrage from a leaf blower.

"Mind your own business. Mister…Mister Marble," she said.

"I think helping a friend is my business."

"Get out of here!" she yelled.

"You're going to let this drunk punch you?" Malachi said. "I'm not."

Mandy started to cry. And at that instant, Malachi heard Alex shriek, "Mom! Mom!"

He had not listened to Malachi and was now pleading with Mandy.

As Malachi shifted his focus toward Alex, Kenny lunged at Malachi and shoved him forcefully toward the door. "Get out of here before I kill you."

Alex screamed, "Mom!"

"You go to your room. Now!" Mandy said.

Malachi shoved a staggering Kenny to the ground. The effort required no more strength than maneuvering a full case of Great Value Bleach from the top of a full skid. He slumped on the floor—like drunks do after the good times have rolled.

Mandy looked at Kenny sprawling on the floor and then at Malachi. "You get out of here or I'm calling the police."

"Mandy, is this what you want? Is living this way better than following Jesus?"

"Malachi leave. Now!"

"You told me when we went out that you didn't like beer or weed."

"Things changed."

"That fast, Mandy?"

"So, I lied. I thought moving to Manistee would change things. You know…I was hoping for a new Mandy."

"There can be a new Mandy. You can be born again."

"Like Stu. Stu-type born again," Mandy said. "Is that what you want for me, Malachi?"

Malachi swallowed hard and shifted his eyes away from

her.

After a few seconds of silence, Mandy said, "When Kenny told me that the God-stuff doesn't work, I knew in my heart he was telling me the truth."

20. The Stalker

"**A**lex, what's wrong!" Malachi nearly screamed three nights later.

There was Alex standing at the end of the aisle, twenty minutes after the shift had begun. Malachi rushed over to him. "What's wrong?"

Alex extended his right hand toward Malachi. "Mom told me to give you this."

He was holding a sealed white envelope. Malachi stared at it for several seconds and then took it from Alex's hand. He held it, intently focusing on the words neatly written on its face. *To: Malachi.*

While Malachi stood there absorbed in his thoughts, Alex said, "Do you have any kids?"

"What…ah…what did you say?"

"Do you have any kids?"

"No. No I don't, Alex?"

"Why not?"

Malachi rubbed the side of his face with his left hand. "Why not?"

Then it happened, unannounced without warning as Malachi was pondering an answer. Alex hugged Malachi around the stomach, briefly pressing his head against his body.

Alex said, "I like you."

Malachi instinctively responded, "I like you too."

And then Alex said, "Mom's waiting in the car." He turned around and left.

Malachi watched Alex as he hurried out of the store. And then he shifted his focus to the envelope in his hand. With his right index finger, he opened the envelope and unfolded the single sheet of off-white, lined, tablet paper.

> Malachi,
> Don't stalk me. Timothy told me you've been by DT's. Do not come to find me at work. I will call the police. Do not call. Do not come by my apartment.
> Mandy

Malachi shook his head as he said in a whisper, "Now I'm stalking her." He searched his brain regarding his visit to DT's and said to himself, "Stalking? How did she come up with that? Because I went to DT's? I actually had a pleasant conversation with Timothy."

Malachi and Timothy knew each other predominately by sight. Only in passing had words traveled between them. Typically, "Hey Timothy. What's up, Malachi," with no expected response of any significance. But they did *know* each other regarding their place in Mandy's life—pretty much.

Timothy was Mandy's boss and the owner of DT's Good

Time Place.

"Hey Timothy."

"What's up, Malachi?"

"I don't see Mandy. Is she around?"

"No, she doesn't...well...ah," Timothy said. And then he motioned his head toward the kitchen area. "You got a minute to talk?"

They made their way back to Timothy's office, a walled-off corner of the kitchen—small, the size of a large walk-in closet.

"Excuse the mess," Timothy said. "Have a seat."

"So, what did you want to talk about?"

"Well ah...Mandy," Timothy said. "Mandy has told me about you. Not much. Just here and there stuff. So, I know you're a good guy, Malachi."

"I try."

Timothy leaned toward Malachi. "I'm very concerned about Mandy. She's...she's...I'm very concerned for her. She's just not...she's...ah...changed. Can you help, Malachi?"

As Malachi pondered his response, Timothy said, "She really thinks a lot of you. I know she'll listen to you."

"I don't know what I can do anymore," Malachi said. And then he updated Timothy on their relational status—the sanctified, abbreviated version. "But I'll do whatever I can."

Already very subdued, Timothy became even more somber. "I've seen this happen over and over again. I hire someone who has just moved to town—trying to make a new start. They make a run at it. And then they crash." He shook his head. "I don't know if I can handle it anymore. I thought Mandy would make it. I thought she was different—in a good way."

Malachi looked at Timothy for a long moment and then said, "You have a soft heart."

As if he hadn't even heard Malachi, he just kept talking. A monologue lasting for several minutes. It kept circling around the same theme—"I should get out of the restaurant business.

I just don't have what it takes anymore. But I can't just walk away. I can't."

Then like an instant change of a television channel, he looked directly at Malachi and measured out his words, "When I was young, the desire of my heart was to own a restaurant. Malachi, make sure you know the desire of your heart is the right desire. Because you know what? Now I'm trapped by what I thought was the desire of my heart."

Malachi stared at Timothy and then said, "That's really profound."

A hint of a smile erased some of the gloom from Timothy's face, "Ah...thanks."

And then Malachi felt his own smile returning. "Timothy, I'm not sure there's much I can do for Mandy. I don't even know what to do. But it does seem to me that you could use a little help in your life."

Timothy nodded.

"Timothy, maybe God sent me to help you."

"Maybe," Timothy said. "Just maybe."

"You should come to Jesus at Walmart."

"Jesus at Walmart?" Timothy said. "Tell me about it as I walk you to the door. I need to get back to work. I have no choice."

As they stood facing each other just inside DT's main door, Malachi said, "You should come by sometime."

"You know, I'm usually up that late anyway," Timothy said. And then his countenance took a couple of down ticks. "You know what, Malachi? I never talk about it anymore, but I used to be really into God."

Malachi cocked his head. "Time for a revival?"

Timothy grinned.

Malachi looked at Carl and said, "I wish Timothy would come to Jesus at Walmart. I really felt a connection with him.

But I never go to DT's. Don't want to be a stalker, you know."

He then shifted his focus, staring for a long time out the side window of the Suburban before saying, "I've never saw Mandy again. Not even once."

They sat there in silence. Several moments passed.

Then Malachi looked back over at Carl. "Aren't you going to say something. You know…tell me why I shouldn't feel so dreadful because of Mandy."

Carl drew in a breath before he said, "Seems like that would be like encouraging a person to 'Get happy' while they were looking into a loved one's casket."

21. The Alex Thing

And then Malachi said, "But at some point…the mourning has to end."

"Should," Carl said.

"Yeah…and now the Alex thing," Malachi said. "I mean… the day I got that phone call..."

Malachi looked at the screen on his cell phone when it rang. Seeing the word, "Mandy," set off a smorgasbord of emotions—from delight to flat-out terror.

He took a breath and put on a happy voice, "Mandy."

"Malachi."

"Hello…ah…," Malachi said. "Oh, this isn't Mandy."

"It's Alex."

"Alex, is everything O.K.?" Malachi blurted into the

phone. "Is your mom…"

"Everything is fine," Alex said. "Really. I mean…well really."

"You sure?"

"I wanted to talk to you. And Mom said it would be O.K."

"She did?" Malachi said. "Are you lying to me? What's wrong?"

"I ah…I wanted to talk."

"About what?"

"I don't know."

"Everything's O.K.?"

"Yeah. Well, you know. Yeah."

"And you just wanted to talk and your mom knows."

"Yeah."

Malachi didn't say anything for a couple of seconds.

And then he heard, "Malachi, do you like to play basketball?"

At that instant, Alex's spur-of-the-moment hug in Walmart flashed into Malachi's mind. Surprised by his own emotions for the boy, along with compassion for his situation and the fact that he genuinely liked Alex, stirred Malachi as he answered.

"I love to play basketball," Malachi said. "Can we play sometime? That would be fantastic."

"Really!"

"Really."

Carl looked over at Malachi. "Got yourself a little buddy."

"Got myself a good friend," Malachi said with a smile on his face as he looked at Carl.

And then he continued, "It's the strangest relationship I've ever been in. I typically do something with Alex once a week. We always have a great time. But I never see Mandy. I don't talk to her—ever. Just Alex. And Alex told me once with sternness—an eleven-year-old's sternness, 'Mom told me that you and I should never talk about her. O.K.?'"

"It's like you're divorced and you have visitation rights."

"But every time I'm with Alex, I want Mandy to be there too," Malachi said. "I don't want to be *divorced*. I don't want that!"

And then he pounded the steering wheel. "I'm still mourning. Mandy is still the desire of my heart."

Malachi abruptly turned his head and stared out the side window again. And then murmured a few decibels over a whisper, "Jump."

22. Happy New Year Malachi

"Malachi, I understand how special Mandy is to you," Carl said. "And of course, I can't fully comprehend…the full spectrum of emotions you're going through. Still I keep thinking, or I should say expecting, that God is…"

Then Carl looked over at Malachi. "What is that?"

"My cell phone," Malachi said. "I just got a new ringtone—*Awesome God.*"

Malachi quickly looked at the screen of his phone. His face lit up like a light bulb. He sat up straighter in his seat and flashed a smile over at Carl.

"It's Elysia," Malachi said.

Carl mouthed the word, "Elysia?"

Malachi waved his hand at Carl and then spoke into the phone, "Hey Elysia."

Carl just grinned as he watched Malachi.

"I'm in town, Malachi," Elysia said. "Thought I should call and wish you a Happy New Year."

"Thank you. Happy New Year to you also," Malachi said. "How long are you going to be in town?"

"I'm not exactly sure. I'm staying at my brother's house—like before. He always wants me to stay longer."

"So, would I…I mean…good to hear your voice," Malachi said as he felt some warmth come to his face. "Yeah…good to hear your voice, Elysia."

"Is everything all right…I ah…you doing O.K?" Elysia said.

Malachi rubbed the left side of his face with his left hand.

"Are you there, Malachi?"

"Elysia, I want to say, 'God is good. Everything is great. Praise God,' and then I would seem like I was really a Godly man. Wouldn't I?"

"Or a phony," Elysia said. "Like God needs another phony Christian roaming planet Earth."

"Here's the deal. The truth—no," Malachi said. "But I'm still alive."

"That's kind of what I was feeling."

"What…what do you mean?"

"When I was praying this morning, your face popped into my head, and God just stirred a feeling in me. Like ah…call Malachi and here's a Bible verse for him."

"Wow. That's cool."

"And here's the verse," Elysia said. "The Lord is near to the brokenhearted. And saves those who are crushed in spirit. Many are the afflictions of the righteous; but the Lord delivers him out of them all. He keeps all his bones. Not one of them is broken."

Malachi's hand holding the phone started to shake. His body quivered like a reed shaking in the wind. He pressed his lips tightly together as his eyes moistened.

"Malachi, are you there? Malachi?" Elysia said. "Can you hear me?"

"Are you there, Malachi?"

"Yeah…yeah. Yeah, I'm here."

"Did that verse mean anything to you?"

Malachi trembled for a few more moments before releasing the words, "Everything. Everything Elysia."

He paused and then, as if to exhale, he said, "God is good."

"Praise God," Elysia said.

He took a deep breath and then said, "It sure is good to hear your voice."

"Yeah, it's good to hear yours too."

"Hey Elysia, there's something I need to ask you. And if I don't ask you right now, I'll feel awful." Malachi glanced over at Carl. "And I might jump off a cliff. Hey…ah…do you want to go out and get a pizza sometime or something like that?"

"If I say no, will you jump off a cliff?"

They both laughed.

"Sure. Pizza sounds great," Elysia said.

As soon as Malachi disconnected the phone, Carl punched him on the shoulder. "You're Mr. Smooth. Date me or I'll jump off a cliff. Really smooth."

Malachi shook his head back and forth with a grin on his face. "Whatever it takes."

And then the words Malachi heard Carl say were like sipping the world's finest hot chocolate, "She's someone special to you. Isn't she?"

They warmed his whole body before he replied, "Yeah. She is."

"I don't ever recall you talking about her, though."

"Remember when I told you about the first time Mandy and I went out," Malachi said, "actually, the only time."

"Who could forget?" Carl said.

"Yeah, I'm telling you about the wonderful time Mandy and I had. I'm falling in love," Malachi said. "And I could tell when I looked at your face it was obvious you weren't getting happy."

"Because I wasn't."

"The words you said are still etched in my mind," Malachi said. "You said, 'Sounds like it's beyond simply eating a couple of sandwiches— hear me out. Because of your wife's unfaithfulness, you can Biblically get a divorce and not be sinning. But you are *still* married. At this point, your relationship with Mandy would have an appearance of evil. And that's not good for anyone.' And then Carl, you really dropped the bomb when you asked me, 'So what would you tell a teenager regarding this type of relationship—a Christian dating a non-Christian? I'm sure you know the Bible verse to cite on this one.'"

Malachi looked directly at Carl. "You were right. I don't know why I wrestled you on something I knew in my heart. And I even tried to wrestle God."

"But you made the right decision," Carl said. "Of course, then you *adjusted* your relationship with Mandy."

"Adjust," Malachi said. "Yeah…that was…challenging."

"It seems like this conversation has drifted off into Mandy-world again," Carl said.

"No. No," Malachi said. "I'm just trying to make a point. Well, my divorce wasn't final yet when I met Elysia. So, I wasn't looking at Elysia as someone to date. And I wasn't going to let myself get askew again in that area of my life."

Carl smiled. "You're learning."

"Yeah," Malachi said. "I guess I didn't tell you about Elysia because I didn't exactly understand our relationship. It's hard to explain. I guess in high school, if you didn't understand algebra, you're not going to be talking about it all the time."

"But you might ask questions."

"I didn't have any questions. What I did have was a sense

that I was honoring God," Malachi said. "Our connection wasn't romantic, and I didn't get drawn to her by her captivating looks. There was nothing flirty or heart fluttering. There were no spiky emotional episodes where I felt, 'Oh I need to tell Carl about this or I'll explode.'"

"It sounds like, in a smooth refined way, you simply became friends. No big headlines."

"Yeah, that's a good way to put it," Malachi said.

Neither one said anything for a bit. Carl could tell Malachi was deep in thought.

"What are you thinking about?" Carl said to break the silence.

"I was thinking about the first time I met Elysia," Malachi said. "I was with Alex."

23. The Elysia Thing

"O.K. Alex, one more round of H.O.R.S.E. and then we'll run on the track," Malachi said. "You know our regular regiment."

Soon, they were jogging around the quarter mile track—nearly touching each other as they ran side by side. "Nice and steady, Alex. Stay relaxed. Pace yourself," Malachi said. "Do you want to see if you can do six laps this week?"

"Six laps?"

"I think you can do it," Malachi said. "We're just here to have fun. Give it a try."

"Yeah," Alex said. "And then I'll time you on your fast mile."

"Yep. You know our routine."

One, two, three, four, five. "O.K. finish strong," Malachi

said. "Excellent. Very good, young man."

Malachi gave Alex a high-five.

And then Alex said, "Give me your watch and I'll time you."

Every summer, Malachi liked to incorporate running timed miles on the track as part of his fitness plan. He would tell people, "You have to exercise your heart. It's your most important muscle." So, through a lot of huffing and puffing, he would push his heart rate to the edge.

As Alex punched the stopwatch, Malachi took off.

The only other person at the track was noticing his straining. As Malachi neared the half-mile mark, she yelled, "Steady." And as he neared the finish line, she yelled again, "You're almost there."

Malachi crossed the finish line in 6:47.

"Wow Malachi, that was your best so far," Alex said.

In a few moments, the woman who was cheering jogged by. "Hey thanks for the encouragement," Malachi said.

She stopped, smiled, "Is this your son?"

Malachi looked over at Alex, "I wish."

Alex got a big grin on his face. "Malachi doesn't have any kids."

Malachi then said to Alex, "We better get going."

He shifted his focus back toward the woman and said, "We'll see you…" He stopped, stood in the momentary silence—as if he was listening for something. And then said, "You're a follower of Jesus, aren't you?"

"All the way."

Malachi extended his hand. "My name is Malachi Marble, and my friend here is Alex Howard."

"Elysia Estellie," she said as they shook hands.

"What a beautiful name."

"Malachi, you're Mr. Charming," Carl said. "Didn't you

tell Mandy she had beautiful fingers the first night you met her? And now it's the *beautiful name* line you're using on Elysia. That's a good one."

Malachi smiled. "It was nothing like that. And meeting Elysia was nothing like when I first met Mandy. When the words *beautiful name* left my lips, I heard a voice in my head, 'The pure in heart shall see God.' I felt this vibe coming from her, a witness in the spirit, like the glory of God emanating... radiating from her. And all I knew was her name and that she was a Believer."

"Yeah," Carl said. "I've experienced that. But not very often—very rarely."

"We kept seeing each other at the track. Mainly smiles, a 'hey' or 'how you doing' maybe a little fellow-runner encouragement. And she was always so sweet to Alex."

Malachi paused, rubbed his chin with his right hand. "It was the second or third time, maybe fourth...no it was the third time, I asked Elysia, 'So how long have you lived in Manistee?'"

"I'm staying with my brother. He's the pastor at Living Water Bible Church," Elysia told me. "I'm a Missionary."

"Interesting," Carl said.

"I wanted to ask her to go with Alex and me to get some ice cream," Malachi said. "Because immediately, I wanted to know everything about her. But I thought to myself, 'No that's too much like a date. Don't do that.'"

Carl nodded his head. "Good decision. And now that legal matters with you and Annie are finalized, from God's perspective, the circumstances have turned. Well, many people...good people, believe differently. Still..."

"Elysia and I had some really nice conversations standing there on the track, just chit chatting over the course of the next few weeks, until she left Manistee," Malachi said. "She's been a missionary essentially her entire adult life. And it seems she's around my age—you know, in her early forties—give or take—it's hard to tell. She's so dedicated in serving Jesus. Guess where she's been serving the last eight years?"

Carl shrugged his shoulders.

"China," Malachi said. "We had an intriguing conversation about China and my own guitar manufacturing and importing exploits. She was familiar with the area where those guitar makers lived—the ones I met when I was there on a missionary trip. And she plays guitar—some."

When he spoke the word *guitar*, it activated a memory. Though somewhat bittersweet, it started pouring out like thick honey from a jar.

He saw himself approaching the guitar hanging on the wall of his home in Freesoil.

Malachi attached life, passion, and sentiment to every element of the instrument. The opaque-black Manchurian ash face projected a stately demeanor. The African rosewood neck promised lithe acoustic tones. The ebony tuners—a delicate artistic statement. He reflected on the hours he spent designing the logo and the headstock. And he would never forget the delight of Liu and Deng when he agreed to work with them on developing the Kerr Creek Guitar. The endeavor never worked. And he recently cut all ties with what he considered a failure, selling off the remaining guitars at way below cost. The little money he did receive helped fund his move from a tent in the Manistee National Forest to his present residence.

And now the only thing that mattered to him was that he still had his own Kerr Creek Guitar, which continued to be a joy in his life—something special.

Even though he was always quick to say, "I'm not very good at playing guitar."

Essentially—he played songs to God.

And this day he followed his normal pattern:

The Elysia Thing

Holy is the Lord
Forever
Lift Him up and worship

King of Kings, and Lord of Lords
Forever

Lift Him up and worship
Worship
Worship Him

Merciful is the Lord
Forever
Lift Him up and worship

King of Kings, and Lord of Lords
Forever

Lift Him up and worship
Worship
Worship Him

Almighty is the Lord
Forever
Lift Him up and worship

King of Kings, and Lord of Lords
Forever

Lift Him up and worship
Worship
Worship Him

Worship
Worship Him

Forever

When he finished, he returned his Kerr Creek Guitar to the bracket on the living room wall. And then he retrieved his Bible from the kitchen table and sat down in the living room. Playing the guitar and singing to God always left him refreshed—feeling closer to God. Always.

As he sat there, sensations of gratitude entered his heart, so much so that he started softly saying, "Praise God. Praise God."

And suddenly, something else entered his heart, "Give your guitar to Elysia."

Malachi gently pushed the feeling away, thinking, "Wow. What an off-the-wall thought."

"Give your guitar to Elysia," returned with more vigor.

Malachi gracefully countered, "That doesn't make any sense."

"The just shall live by faith. Give your guitar to Elysia," pressed against his emotions, like an intruder trying to muscle open a shut door.

Malachi dug in his resolve for a week or two.

Until.

Until, one day when Alex said to him as they neared the Suburban after a track workout, "We should give Elysia a gift. She's so nice."

Malachi looked at Alex. "What makes you say that?"

"I don't know," Alex said. "When you were talking to her, it was like my brain tuned into a voice…kind of in my head and it said, 'Give Elysia a gift. Something special.' That's all that happened."

"That's all?"

"Yeah," Alex said. "That's all."

Malachi turned his head when Carl said, "Elysia plays guitar? Have you heard her play?"

"Only once. At the track one day."

"At the track?" Carl said.

"Yeah," Malachi said. "But that's ah…kind of…another story."

24. The Call

"Is that *Awesome God* calling you again?" Carl said.

"I never get this many calls," Malachi said.

"Hey Malachi, Happy New Year."

"Thanks. Same to you, my friend," Malachi said. "So how are you doing?"

"I have been crucified with Christ and it is no longer I who live, but Christ lives in me. And the life which I now live in the flesh I live by faith in the Son of God, who loved me and gave Himself up for me," Martin said. "Galatians 2:20."

Malachi smiled. But inside he was saying, "Oh Lord, don't let Martin crash and burn." There were no noticeable signs. But Malachi felt uneasy as his mind drifted back to the night when Martin first found out about Jesus at Walmart.

"Hey Martin."

"What's up, Malachi?"

"You're creative. If you were going to have a get together here at Walmart—during lunchtime to talk about the Bible and Jesus and how all this ties into everyday life, what would be a good name?"

"Hmm? Let me see. You'll be talking about Jesus and the Bible and stuff...and life and working at Walmart...and how it all connects together. Hmm? How about *Jesus at Walmart*?"

"I like it. I think God just gave us the perfect name. Would you come?"

"Maybe. Is there free food?"

"Spiritual food."

"Does it give you heartburn?" Martin said.

"Heartburn," Malachi said to himself with his cell phone pressed against his ear. The man, who jokingly was concerned that spiritual food might cause heartburn, now had an almost insatiable appetite for the things of God. And then Malachi thought, "I hope he doesn't get derailed—he's going so fast." And then he shook his head. "I've seen it happen before."

"Malachi? You still there?"

"Yeah," Malachi said. "Happy New Year, Martin."

"What?" Martin said.

"Just thinking about something. Thinking about...ah... what God is doing in your life."

"Praise God," Martin said. "Hey, the reason I'm calling is ah...well, I'm not sure I'm allowed to do this. I hope it's O.K. I mean, I'm just a regular guy."

"What is it, Martin?"

"When I read through Leviticus yesterday..."

"You read through the book of Leviticus yesterday—in one day?"

"It only took about four hours...well, that's with taking a

few pages of notes," Martin said. "It's what I like to do—if I can make the time."

"Wow. That's a lot of commitment."

"I don't know," Martin said. "JC and I watched a movie on Netflix about John Wycliffe. He gave up everything to get the Bible translated into English so the common people could read it. The corrupt church leaders were so angry that forty years after he died, they dug up his bones and burned them. They hated him for getting the word of God out. And another man, John Hess, was burned at the stake for doing the same thing. So, reading the Bible for a few hours seems spineless by comparison. Now those guys, they paid the cost."

"Yeah. I see that. They sure did," Malachi said.

"O.K. back to why I called," Martin said. "When I saw this in the Bible, 'It shall be a holy convocation for you and you shall humble your souls and present an offering by fire to the Lord.' I was like, 'Yeah, that's what I want. Let's do it.'"

"Holy convocation?" Malachi said.

"Can I ah…let's see…" Martin said. "I mean, can we have one?"

Malachi smiled. "Will it cause heartburn?"

"Yes! Yes! Yes! Exactly," Martin said. "Just like in the Bible, when Jesus spoke to the two disciples as they walked on the road to Emmaus, 'They said to one another, 'Were not our hearts burning within us while He was speaking to us on the road, while He was explaining the Scriptures to us?' Yes. That's what we want. Right?"

"Slow down, Martin," Malachi said. "So, what is this *Holy Convocation* you're talking about?"

"O.K. here's the plan. It's simple. Something JC and I came up with yesterday," Martin said. "I want to have a few people, very few, over to my place to humble our souls before God. To present an offering to God—our lives. It will be our way to jump…to jumpstart our relationship with Jesus to a new level as we launch into a new year. Are you ready to jump, Malachi—to a higher level?"

Malachi tried to grapple with some inner wrestling as Martin talked on. He wrestled more than ever when Martin coasted to a stop after several minutes. "No wimps. Got it. Are you in, Malachi?"

"Hey, you know I'm in. Yep. Sure am. I'm in, Martin," Malachi said. Then he turned his head to the left. His visual focus was through the window—all the way to Lake Michigan in the distance. He sighed. His left index finger brushed against his lips. Even Carl, who was sitting to his right, couldn't hear what he whispered, "No wimps."

"Are you there, Malachi?" Martin said.

"Yeah. Yeah. I'm in."

"What did you say? Speak up."

"I'm in...yep."

"You said, 'You're in?'" Martin said. "Is that right?"

"Sure. Yep."

"Great! Remember: Tuesday at my place. 5:00," Martin said. "Can you get a hold of Carl? Invite him. And if you know anyone else, bring them along. No wimps—got it?"

25. No Wimps

Malachi set his cell phone down on the Suburban's console and looked over at Carl. "I feel like a wimp—especially after talking with Martin."

"What do you mean?"

"Compared to Martin," Malachi said. "Yesterday he read the entire book of Leviticus and took notes. Thinks it's what every Christian does. Then he wants to call a Holy Convocation. And here I am—the yoyo Christian. The wimp."

"Comparing yourself to Martin? So that's going to make things better?" Carl said. "You know, Malachi, *comparing* is a downer when you're following Jesus. God's math works differently than ours."

"Well…yeah," Malachi said. "I'm sure it does."

"Let me do some comparing," Carl said, "even though I just

nixed the practice. Martin is in the sweet, newness of his relationship with Jesus. You're a tested veteran, who has just gone through a tough year. Really tough. Plus, your personalities are…let's just say—not apples to apples."

"Yeah. O.K.," Malachi said. "Those are good points."

"Also, Martin has different gifting than you. He studies the Bible with that kind of intensity because he is almost definitely gifted in teaching. Sure, we all need to be serious students of the Word, but Martin is growing in his gift."

"Yeah. I see that."

"You should be celebrating what is happening to Martin, not comparing. He's your fruit. The fruit of you using your gifting," Carl said. "That's one of the main reasons we serve God. And look at JC—praise God. Even through your struggles, God is producing eternal fruit."

"Well thanks, Carl."

"Think about this, Malachi," Carl said. "Wouldn't it be wonderful if Martin eventually zoomed way, way beyond you in ministry? The way he's going—who knows what God might do. Maybe you'll be Martin's Barnabas."

"Martin's Barnabas?" Malachi said.

"In Acts 11 it tells about a revival breaking out in Antioch," Carl said. "The main church leaders sent Barnabas there basically to take charge of what was happening."

"O.K. I remember that."

"And the Bible says, 'Barnabas was a good man, full of the Holy Spirit and faith, and a great number were brought to the Lord,'" Carl said. "It appears the revival kicked up a notch. So, what does Barnabas do?"

"Ah…let me think," Malachi said. "I don't remember."

"Most people miss this," Carl said. "'Then Barnabas went to Tarsus to look for Paul.' Think about what just happened? Barnabas, the big player in the revival, left to go find Paul, who was essentially off the backside of the desert with no ministry going on, in obscurity—probably waiting on God. Barnabas brought Paul back to Antioch to get him involved in ministry, involved in the revival."

"Yeah. I've never seen it that way before. And then not long down the road, Paul totally eclipsed Barnabas in ministry," Malachi said.

"Exactly," Carl said. "God is using you. Significant ministry is flowing from your life. And when you told me about your relationship with Alex—it so warmed my heart. You know, it seems like you don't even think of that as serving God."

"I ah…"

"Let me say something first," Carl said. "That's because in many ways, serving God simply flows out of you. And you're not even aware of it."

"I never thought of it that way."

"I'm thinking, if I talked to Elysia, she would tell me you're a blessing in her life. I just know it."

He then turned and looked intently at Malachi. "You need to quit…quit…"

With an abrupt silence, Carl shifted his gaze toward the windshield.

"Quit?" Malachi said. "Quit what?"

When he didn't respond, Malachi's eyes studied the right side of Carl's face. That's when he noticed a twitching quiver move across Carl's profile.

"Quit…," Carl said as he continued staring ahead. His words pushed off slower and softer. In a measured tone, "I've had plenty of my own weak moments. Even those times when jumping seemed alluring. So alluring."

"Quit." He shook his head, "It's shameful to have to remember those times. And then…to have to own them. Once I was…I was…it was a bad time for me. I…I..."

He was silent for several seconds before he spoke, "I ah…"

And then a single tear trickled down the left side of his face as he began to sing:

> I need Thee every hour, most gracious Lord
> No tender voice like Thine can peace afford
>
> I need Thee, Oh I need Thee
> Every hour I need Thee
> Oh bless me now my Savior
> I come to Thee
>
> I need Thee every hour, stay Thou nearby
> Temptations lose their power when Thou art nigh
>
> I need Thee, Oh I need Thee
> Every hour I need Thee
> Oh bless me now my Savior
> I come to Thee
>
> I need Thee every hour, in joy or pain
> Come quickly and abide, or life is in vain
>
> I need Thee, Oh I need Thee
> Every hour I need Thee
> Oh bless me now my Savior
> I come to Thee
>
> I come to Thee

When his singing ended, silence filled the void, like the sacred moment after a twenty-one-gun salute has sounded.

Then Carl turned toward Malachi. Their visual interaction pushed through the stillness even before Carl's first words.

"God put that old hymn into my spirit at that black, dark time...when I was...asking myself if life was in vain."

A hint of a smile formed on Carl's face. "Before that bleak hour years ago, I hadn't thought of that song or sang it in five, maybe ten years. But when I sang, 'I need Thee. Oh I need Thee,' at the crux of my darkness, my life had changed. By the time I finished the song, God had touched me. He transformed my life."

He paused for a few moments before continuing, "There's no way to explain how it happened...I mean, through human reasoning. It doesn't make a lot of sense. But God...oh I love God...He knew just what I needed for a breakthrough in my life. And my Father in Heaven knew when I needed it."

Malachi slowly nodded.

"I need to caution you, though," Carl said. "Yeah, that breakthrough came like a rushing wind into my spirit, but I had to pay a price to get to the tipping point. Pain, submission to God, calling out to God—but we all arrive uniquely to where God needs us to be. And we never know how or when God might do a life changing work in our lives—a breakthrough."

Carl focused intently on Malachi. "Am I making any sense?"

"Yeah, I see it. You're making perfect sense," Malachi said. "I need my own breakthrough. I definitely need one. Yeah...a breakthrough."

Carl placed his left hand on Malachi's right shoulder. Malachi saw a sparkle in his eye as he prayed, "Dear Father God, like it says in Acts 2:2—'And suddenly.' Amen."

26. Breakthrough

"**C**ongratulations on your breakthrough, Malachi," Sal said.

As Malachi drew in a breath, it smelled like a blend of orange peels and the interior of old running shoes.

"I said congratulations," Sal said.

"Breakthrough. Yeah," Malachi said.

"You seem a little out of it," Sal said as her eyes quickly scrutinized Malachi's face. "You're not the partying type? I mean…after yesterday's shift…you wouldn't go out partying to celebrate the New Year…you know, like some of the call-ins."

"No," Malachi laughed. "I spent most of the first three hours after work sitting in my Suburban talking to a good friend. And then, once I got home, I read my Bible and stuff like that for a…well, I didn't get enough sleep."

Malachi and Sal stood in the ten-foot-by-ten-foot pas-sageway leading to the backroom of the Walmart store. This was day one of his new position at Walmart. ICS—Inventory Control Specialist.

"Well, you need to get your Bible reading and all that out of your mind for now and get focused," Sal said. "This is the first day of your new job—with a nice raise. It's a New Year. You've made it to the next level here at Walmart. I would call that a breakthrough."

At that moment, Malachi's ears and brain were not cogni-zant of the fact that Sal had received a call on her talkie.

Or that after a brief conversation with the person on the other end, she said, "Malachi, I have a little emergency, a *situation*, to deal with. Wait right here."

And off she darted.

The backroom—this is the warehouse area of the store. Directly ahead, six banks of eight-foot tall super-duty metal shelving units were packed with excess inventory. And at the far wall, shelves reached all the way to the bottom of the room's steel trussed ceiling—twelve feet above. Where the walls peaked through the merchandise, raw drywall with taped joints completed the decor.

To Malachi's right were three steel plated loading docks. And around the next wall was a six-foot wide steel roll-up door for receiving vendors, flanked by an industrial gray, welded-steel desk—built for abuse and serious business.

Through casual observation, the placing of goods on the shelves seemed random and haphazard. Though the opposite was actually the case in this area half the size of a basketball court.

Even though there were thousands of items on the shelves, the store's computer knew right where every item was located. An ICS associate affixed barcodes to every carton of merchandise before placing it on the shelves. All the shelves were sequenced to the groupings of merchandise out on the sales floor. Baby food had its section of shelves. Stationary Department's inventory had its home in the warehouse. As did every other store department.

Malachi's new duties involved directing the flow of goods arriving in semis. He would unload the pallets from the trailers with a lift truck. And from there, he would *down stack* the skids. This procedure involved sorting the randomly stacked skids and restacking the goods according to their final destination—aisle or store department. ICS associates usually placed merchandise on rocket carts—a four-wheel cart that resembled a chrome tubular shelving unit—with no top shelf. While larger merchandise and selected items went out on the sales floor on skids pulled by a pallet jack.

The shelves looming in front of Malachi contained items that had gone out onto the sales floor to be stocked, but there was not enough room for the merchandise on the store's shelves. The stockers then returned this merchandise to the warehouse, and it would be designated as overstock. ICS workers would then tag the items with barcodes and systematically place them on the backroom shelves.

And then when the computer system determined that shelving space in the store had opened up, via barcoding at the checkout counter, it communicated to the ICS personnel to retrieve the inventory, re-cart it, and pull it back out to the sales floor for stocking.

The store's computer *talks* to ICS associates via a piece of equipment, called a Telxon. This resembles a ray gun from a science fiction movie. But it is essentially a hand-held PC connected to the store's computer system via a secure Wi-Fi system. Every night, the small palm size screen displayed long lists of merchandise to be moved out of the warehouse. These items were referred to as *picks,* because the computer had *picked* the merchandise from the warehouse's overstock inventory.

The job was fast-paced and sometimes tense. It was common for overstock to be flowing into the backroom from the sales floor before the ICS workers had delivered all the picks out to the stockers.

And like all areas of the store, Sal demanded excellence.

When Sal had said the words, "I would call that a breakthrough," it was as if she had flicked the on switch in Malachi's head for a large scrolling sign, like the one out on the highway which announces, "20% OFF ON ALL PREMIUM DOG FOOD" or the one that entices, "ALL YOU CAN EAT FISH THIS FRIDAY."

Malachi could feel an inner trembling as Words from Scriptures he had read earlier in the day vigorously emanated in his brain. He slumped to his knees as the panorama unfurled:

> I waited patiently for the Lord's help. Then He listened to me and heard my cry. He pulled me out of a dangerous pit—out of the deadly quicksand. He set me safely on a rock and made me secure.
>
> He taught me to sing a new song. A song of praise to our God. Many who see this will take warning and will put their trust in the Lord.
>
> Blessed are those who trust the Lord, who do not turn to idols or join those who worship false gods.
>
> You have done many things for us, O Lord our God. There is no one like You! You have made many wonderful plans for us. I could never speak of them all—their number is so great!
>
> You do not want sacrifices and offerings. You do not ask for animals burned whole on the altar or for sacrifices to take away sins. Instead, You have given me ears to hear

You and so I answered, "Here I am;" Your instructions for me are in the Book of the Law. How I love to do Your will, my God! I keep Your teaching in my heart.

In the assembly of all your people, Lord, I told the Good News that You save us. You know that I will never stop telling it. I have not kept the news of salvation to myself. I have always spoken of Your faithfulness and help. In the assembly of all Your people I have not been silent about Your loyalty and constant love.

I know You will never stop being merciful to me. Your love and loyalty will always keep me safe.

I am surrounded by many troubles—too many to count! My sins have caught up with me and I can no longer see. They are more than the hairs of my head and I have lost my courage.

Save me, Lord! Help me now!

May those who try to kill me be completely defeated and confused. May those who are happy because of my troubles be turned back and disgraced. May those who make fun of me be dismayed by their defeat.

May all who come to You be glad and joyful. May all who are thankful for Your salvation always say, "How great is the Lord!"

I am weak and poor, O Lord, but You have not forgotten me. You are my Savior and my God.

Malachi's body quivered. The words pulsated with life and meaning. At that moment, the theology behind, "For the Word of God is living and active and sharper than any two-edged sword," needed no explanation. Like pulling back the curtains after four days of continual rainy gloom and discovering the view was from the top of Mt. Everest on the crystal clearest day in history, Malachi's mind, his soul, saw more lucidly than ever before.

It was all happening as he kneeled on the concrete of the warehouse floor as waves of warmth and peace traversed through his body—nearly taking his breath away.

After an unknown passing of time, Malachi feebly stood up and raised his hands above his head and proclaimed, "How great is the Lord…. how great is the Lord."

And then he heard Sal say, "What are you…Malachi, I'm back…ah…thanks for your patience. Things come up sometimes. And I need to deal with them. But now I'm back."

"You left?" Malachi said.

Sal looked directly at Malachi. "What's wrong…are you…?"

"I just had a breakthrough," Malachi said. "How great is the Lord."

"Yeah…ah…yeah," Sal said.

"Yeah," Malachi said. "How great is the Lord. I am weak and poor, O Lord, but You have not forgotten me. You are my Savior and my God."

"I've ah…" Sal said. "I've never seen anybody get so…so emotional about a new position at Walmart."

Malachi fought the urge to hug her as he sensed another wave of exuberance when the words Carl had spoken the previous day hit his brain, "You never know how or when God might do a life changing work in our lives—a breakthrough."

27. Holy Convocation

Malachi met Carl at their usual pick up spot. The day had turned much colder than the previous one. Still, Carl was sitting on the black, rolled-steel bench in front of Walmart.

"You look happy," Carl said as they exited the parking lot.

"I am."

"I don't need to ask why," Carl said. "Because we both know Christians are always happy."

"Always."

"Yep. Always," Carl said with a smirk on his face.

Malachi headed the Suburban north on U.S. 31 and said, "Holy Convocation, here we come."

The road veered noticeably to the east as they sat quietly and comfortably together. The air flow from the heater had a hint of wet-wool smell blended with the warmth.

No one said anything until Malachi turned right onto Coates Highway as they headed due east. "Martin lives out in Brethren," Malachi said. "So, the brethren and sistren are gathering in Brethren tonight."

"You sure are happy tonight, Malachi."

"Always."

Carl laughed.

"I invited Elysia to join us tonight," Malachi said. "She was busy."

"Is she's still going to go out with you?"

"I didn't mention it…I mean," Malachi said. "I'm usually shy about…ah…you know…asking for a date."

"But you're a happy shy. Right?"

"O.K. Quit it, Carl."

And then Carl turned and looked at Malachi. "You had a breakthrough. Didn't you?"

"God so amazed me. I'm still just soaking in it all."

"Let it soak in. We can talk about it when you're ready. If ever."

"How did you know?"

Carl laughed. "I've needed many breakthroughs in my days. Most of the time, the really special ones need to hover around your soul before you share them."

Malachi glanced at Carl and nodded his head.

And in a few minutes, they entered the tiny burg of Brethren.

"I've never been to Martin's house," Malachi said. "It should be coming up. There's the pizza place—Uzeppis. And then he lives next door."

He slowed the Suburban and said, "O.K., here we are."

When the door opened, Martin had a big smile on his face. Malachi couldn't help thinking, "And this is the person whose routine facial expression used to reflect a depressed demeanor and a negative outlook."

"Malachi…Carl. Come in. Thank you for joining us this fine evening."

When Malachi stepped in the door, he said, "It smells nice in here."

"Those are apple-cinnamon candles JC bought me for Christmas," Martin said. "Guess where she bought them?"

They laughed.

And then Malachi heard a familiar voice, "Malachi."

"Elysia."

"I didn't know you knew Martin."

"We go to Living Water Bible Church now," JC said as she entered the room. "Elysia's brother is the Pastor there. You two know each other?"

"Yeah," Malachi said.

"We sort of ran into each other," Elysia said as she smiled.

"We met at the Manistee High School track," Malachi said.

"Why don't we all have a seat? Get comfortable," Martin said.

As Martin circled his eyes around those gathered, his countenance shifted. And then he said very quietly to JC, who was sitting beside him on an orange and brown striped couch, "Will the food be O.K. until later? I don't think I can eat anything right now."

"It'll be fine," she replied softly.

He looked across at Malachi, who was semi-sunken into an over-stuffed chair with a bold woodland scene on the upholstery. Next, he shifted his focus to Carl, whose arm covered most of the rip on the armrest of a well-worn beige recliner. And finally, he glanced over at Elysia, who had edged up against the other arm of the sofa.

"It feels weird to me to be leading the meeting tonight…I mean, you all are such amazing followers of Jesus. But I'm not going to deny what God has stirred in me and JC."

No one said anything. And with only a brief halt, Martin continued, "It would probably seem more Godly, I guess, if I could say I was reading the Bible when the initial thoughts stirred in me for this...ah...what I'm calling a Holy Convocation. But that's not what happened."

Martin looked directly at Malachi. "I hope I'm doing O.K."

"I'm already starting to feel the presence of God," Malachi said. "Keep going."

"There's this book I was reading," Martin said. "It talked about people in China."

His eyes met Elysia's. And then he continued, "The book was telling about the cost people in China have paid to be followers of Jesus. Suffering...some would even die for their faith."

Elysia nodded her head.

Martin's facial muscles tensed as he continued, "It seemed so bizarre because a page or so later, the book talked about an office worker in Texas who was brown-bagging it. And the money he saved by not going out to lunch, he was sending to missionaries, which is great. But the point the book was making was that the office worker was paying a cost—I mean, like suffering. In China, people are dying for Jesus, and in the United States, we eat peanut butter and jelly sandwiches for Jesus."

He looked around the room again. "That's stupid. It was a good book...really good. But when..."

Martin folded his arms. His eyes turned away from the group. And he was silent for several moments. He drew in a deep breath and returned his focus to those gathered. "I just couldn't shake the contrast. It just burrowed into my soul. And then...and then JC had her dream...it kind of," he swallowed hard, "kind of...broke...me."

Holy Convocation

JC's eyes fell to the floor. And then she slowly raised her head.

> Wow. It was weird.
>
> There were two parts.
>
> In the first part, I was stocking at Walmart… imagine that. I was stocking some crosses. They were around seven inches tall. With shiny, chrome edging—enough so I could see my reflection. The center part of the crosses was black. And there was a silvery Jesus hanging on the black part.
>
> When I slapped the pricing gun on the first cross, a regular pricing sticker didn't come out of the gun—there wasn't a number on the pricing label, just vibrant red letters that said, *The Cost*, which was doubly strange, because I knew the gun only had black ink in it.
>
> I then moved the knob on the side of the pricing gun to double check the price and slapped the gun again. Again, it came out red, *The Cost*. So, I slapped it several more times. Same thing happened.
>
> And then instantly—the second part of the dream started—I was overlooking a church service. And Jesus, who had a resemblance to the one on the cross, now had a pricing gun in His hand, the one I had been holding.
>
> In the dream, I was looking over His shoulder. Sort of attached to Jesus—kind of.
>
> I didn't recognize anyone or the church. As we went up and down the aisle, Jesus just walked past almost everybody—maybe because they totally ignored Him. And then there were a few people who Jesus attempted to affix pricing stickers on. But they prevented Him by raising their hands or pushing the gun away. Or they used their Bibles to fend off Jesus.

The service just kept going on, like Jesus wasn't there. There were probably about three-hundred people at the church. Jesus even went up to the pastor. He pushed Jesus away. It was kind of bizarre when the guy playing guitar and leading the music used the guitar to avoid the pricing gun. He used it like a ping-pong paddle to swat the pricing gun away.

And then I saw myself. Jesus was coming toward me, and He lifted the pricing gun and all I could think of was, *The Cost.*

Then the dream ended.

Elysia's face contorted, as tears trickled onto her blouse.

JC shifted her position on the couch and hugged her. She held her for several minutes.

And when Elysia regained her composure she said, "Yesterday, I had something happen to me; that had never happened to me before...at least not like that."

"I..." She said and then pressed her lips together. She looked upward and then refocused on the group.

I had...I guess I have to call it a vision...or something like that. I was up in the bedroom at my brother's house—the bedroom I always stay in. There's a chair in the room, and I was reading my Bible and pondering the things of God, offering some prayers as people and situations came to mind.

Suddenly, pictures started appearing—almost like a movie. But there were no borders to the screen.

It was so vivid that I can still see it clearly in my mind. Pictures of different churches kept appearing. None that I recognized. It must have been on a Sunday because all the parking lots had generous amounts of vehicles in them.

That seemed normal. The signage was what jumped out at me. I can still see the words on those church signs: Low Price Guarantee. Price Reduced. We Will Not be Undersold. No Reasonable Offer Refused. Free to a Good Home. Lowest Prices in the State. Make an Offer We Can't Refuse. Easy Payment Plan.

And then at the last church, I saw in my vision, Jesus was standing outside wearing a sandwich sign. Walking back and forth. There were only two cars in the parking lot.

I saw very clearly the words on His sign, "Anyone who loves his father or mother more than Me is not worthy of Me. Anyone who loves his son or daughter more than Me is not worthy of Me. And anyone who does not take up his cross and follow Me is not worthy of Me. Whoever finds his life will lose it and whoever loses his life for My sake will find it."

And then the vision ended.

No one said anything for a couple of minutes.

Malachi felt his heart beating in his chest as his eyes slowly scanned the somber group.

Then JC said, "My dream kind of frightened me."

"What I experienced seemed so real," Elysia said.

Malachi, once again, became aware of his heart throbbing as silence returned to the room.

Until Carl broke the hush, like leaves crackling in a dead-still forest, "Can I say something?"

"Sure."

"Yeah."

"Please."

"In Deuteronomy, I believe it's 19:15, we're told, 'By the mouth of two or three witnesses a matter shall be established.' So, three people have spoken out on the same, almost exact theme. And just a couple of days ago, Malachi and I talked at length and this was a significant thread in our discussion also."

Carl looked over at Malachi. They both hesitated. Like that split-second glance of indecision basketball players give each other. Should I pass the ball? Are you going to pass the ball?

"I ah…" Martin said. "That was really good, Carl. Do you have something you want to say, Malachi? Carl?"

"Seems like it's time to pass the ball back to you," Malachi said.

"I was reading in Leviticus recently. I came across these words," Martin said as he picked up his Bible. "'It shall be a holy convocation for you and you shall humble your souls and present an offering by fire to the Lord.' That's where I… that's when God stirred my heart specifically to have this get-together—this holy convocation."

He looked over at JC and then at Elysia and continued around the circle as he set his gaze on Malachi and finally Carl.

And then he spoke, "Wouldn't it be appropriate for followers of Jesus Christ to gather at the beginning of each year to sound the trumpet, declaring their commitment to shake off spiritual drowsiness? Declaring their commitment to searching their hearts and intently examining their ways—their manner of living and declaring their commitment to make amends before a Holy God. A humbling of our souls before our Lord. Our Savior. Our King.

Martin extended his hands, turning his palms upward. He looked at his palms and then peered heavenward. "What offering can we bring to God? What could we—with humble hearts, with eager hearts, present to God at the dawn of a New Year?"

Martin fell to his knees and bowed his head.

And JC and Elysia were sobbing before the next words came out of his mouth, "Father God, I bring my offering to You. Whatever the cost, whatever it takes to follow you, I pick up my cross. I will follow you My Lord—no cost is too great."

By then, Malachi was kneeling with his face buried in the chair he had been sitting on. Carl's body was sprawled out on the floor. His face hard against the carpet.

The room was filled with voices making declarations and commitments to God. No one seemed to be conscious of anyone else. Expressions of repentance flowed. Sounds of weeping crested and ebbed.

The awareness of time blurred.

And one by one, composure was regained, but no one was concerned about what tears had done to their appearance or the reduced neatness of their attire.

Martin was the first to say anything, "Praise God. Praise God."

A resounding chorus of, "Praise God!" saturated the atmosphere.

And then Martin stood and said, "We need to gather in a prayer circle to set our resolve and to symbolize our united stand in the commitments and declarations we've made tonight." At that, everyone flowed to the center of the room and embraced.

"Father God," Martin said. "In Your Word it says, 'Two people can resist an attack that would defeat one person alone. A rope made of three cords is hard to break.' Help us to be a cord of five strands—strong and mighty to do exploits for Your kingdom. Help us to stand with each other in our declarations and commitments. In all, we know, 'It's not by power; it's not by might, but by My Spirit says the Lord.' So, we ask and believe for an extra measure of the Holy Spirit, as we give You our offerings—lives willing to pay the cost to be fully devoted followers of Jesus Christ. Amen."

"Amen."
"Amen."
"Amen."
"Amen."

28. Coffee Anyone?

"I'm thinking maybe a Holy Convocation might mean ah…might include fasting," Martin said "…but hey, JC thank you for making the food. And we thank You God for this food. Give us strength to honor You. Amen."

A few minutes after everyone had returned to the living room and were relaxing with their refreshments, Martin looked attentively at JC with a smile on his face. They focused on each other, and Martin said in a hushed tone, "Now."

JC nodded her head as her face brightened.

"Hey everyone, we…ah have something we want you to know," Martin said. "God has done an amazing work in my heart and in JC's heart. And by what seems like God's hand, JC and I have traveled the spiritual road together, the road to knowing Jesus as our Savior and beyond.

He then reached over and caressed JC's hand. "We are now launching into a God-honoring dating relationship—we're courting. We've been reading everything we can find in the Bible about…ah…relationships. And we're talking to Elysia's brother—Pastor Gordy."

He turned toward JC. They gazed into each other's eyes. "We're hoping this journey takes us to marriage."

Instantly, the other three burst into applause, "Yea!"

Martin and JC stood up holding hands and took a bow.

And then they clapped again.

When everyone settled down, Malachi sipped his coffee and directed his visual attention toward Martin and JC as they sat near each other. At that moment, he suppressed an intense wave of emotions as tears came to his eyes. A pleasant warmth enveloped his body as he said in an undetectable whisper, "You are so awesome, God. So awesome."

He then glanced over at Elysia. "Was she looking at me?" he thought. Their eyes met for the briefest of moments. And they both quickly turned away.

"Malachi," Martin said. "Let me show you my music room. I know you play guitar."

"Sure."

"Elysia? Carl? Want a quick tour?" Martin said.

"Yeah. That would be great," Elysia said.

"I'm pretty comfortable just sitting here," Carl said.

Elysia and Malachi followed Martin down the hallway. He turned right into the last bedroom, just past the bathroom.

"Wow," Malachi said as he entered the room.

There was a bass guitar, electric guitar, and an acoustic guitar lined up on stands along the wall to the right. Off to the left of a window, which was directly ahead, was a two-tiered keyboard. And to the right and on the next wall were shelves with a variety of musical accoutrements. Three amps on the lower shelves. Mikes. Mike stands, music books, various electronic components, and an encased instrument. Malachi figured it was a saxophone—because he knew Martin played saxophone.

And then off to the left of the door, two feet out from the wall, was a stool, twenty-four inches tall. The well-worn blue wood seat was carved in contours to match a human's bottom—supported by stout light red legs and horizontal bracing.

Of everything in the room, Malachi's eyes were drawn to a mandolin hanging on the wall above the stool.

Martin noticed his attentiveness and said, "You can play it. Go ahead."

"I've never seen one up close."

Martin removed it from the bracket and placed it in Malachi's awaiting hands.

"This is beautiful," Malachi said. "It seems so small."

Half the size of a guitar, the teardrop-shaped body had an oval shaped sounding hole the size of an extra-large egg. The body was tobacco brown, which became darker toward the perimeter. The ebony toned neck had a medium brown accent line along the edge. The eight tuners were veined, pearl white.

"It's really cool looking," Malachi said. "I've never tried to play one."

"Go ahead."

Malachi ran his thumb over the strings. "It has a nice sound. Really nice."

Martin smiled. "We usually use a pick. But I did see a movie about U2 recording the Joshua Tree album, and in it, a guy strummed a mandolin with his thumb. They called the technique *scrape*."

He then showed Malachi three main chords—the two-finger version of the chords. And then Malachi began strumming them.

"You sound good. You got the beat. You're hitting those chords nicely," Martin said. "You want to try a pick?"

"No, that's O.K.," Malachi said. "I like the way it sounds with my thumb."

"I rarely touch my mandolin," Martin said. "It just hangs there on the wall."

"I always thought my fingers were the wrong size to play the guitar," Malachi said. "You know—too thick. But I can play the chords on a smaller instrument. What's the deal?"

"Malachi, I saw a guy on YouTube, with no arms, playing the guitar—with his feet. Sure, there are guys with ideal fingers. But it usually doesn't work out that way. It just doesn't."

Martin shook his head. "I don't know why. Remember what you said to me once, 'God uses the foolish to confound the wise.' And for some reason, your foolish fingers got it going on with that mandolin."

Malachi smiled. And so did Elysia, who had been observing what was happening.

Martin then stood motionless for several seconds. He stared unfocused—off to the right of Malachi. And then he looked directly at him. "I want you to have the mandolin. It's yours—on one condition—you always honor God with it—with the music."

"I can't take your mandolin."

"So, you help me get my soul saved, and I can't give you a $400 hunk of wood, plastic, and metal, which I haven't played in two years," Martin said. "I'm thinking it's the Book of Acts thing, you know, 'The group of believers was one in mind and heart. None of them said that any of their belongings were their own, but they all shared with one another everything they had.'"

Malachi hugged Martin. "Thank you so much. I ah… thank you so much."

When Malachi stepped back from the embrace, he heard Elysia say, "Man of God."

He turned and looked into her eyes; she smiled and said

softly, "Man of God. For whatever a man sows, that shall he also reap."

29. Leap

When Malachi walked into Walmart at 9:52 the next night, so many thoughts were jostling through his mind, "Now what?"

The contrast between working through the night at Walmart and the Holy Convocation at Martin's seemed glaring. Overwhelming. Unsettling.

He said to himself, "The talk needs to become the walk."

In his mind, he kept musing over a snippet of scripture, one Martin had spoken the previous evening just before everyone departed. It referenced John the Baptist, "John was a burning and a shining light."

And then Martin had offered a charge to the group, "This year, let us be a burning and shining light for Jesus Christ."

Malachi thought to himself as he made his way to the time

clock, "But not a glaring, irritating light, like a LED flashlight directly in the eyes."

After the nightly worker's meeting, Malachi quickly made his way to his new station. The backroom.

As he entered the work area, he thought to himself, "I wish JC was here." When Malachi started at Walmart eight months prior, JC worked in the backroom. She recently had moved to first shift with a promotion to Zone Manager—a manager over three departments. And even Spencer, another familiar face in the backroom, had moved on with a transfer to the Cadillac store thirty-six miles east of Manistee.

A new hire, Dotty, was Malachi's coworker in the warehouse area. And thinking about all the changes was quickly bumped out of his mind as his eyes perused the Telxon screen.

He looked up at Dotty, who was doing the same thing. "Wow, we have a lot of picks tonight."

"Yeah," Dotty said. "We sure do."

As they divvied up tasks and formed a game plan, Malachi was thinking, "I've never invited Dotty to Jesus at Walmart."

He glanced back down at his Telxon screen and said to himself, "At break."

The race was on. With nearly three hundred picks from eighteen different departments, it was a challenging workload. And they didn't have all night to complete the list because at exactly 3:00 A.M., the Telxon screen would blip to white. The store's main computer wiped the list away like an erasure on a chalkboard—gone.

3:00 A.M. was the finish line banner for the Inventory Control Specialist, at least for the first race of the night.

Malachi marched into the shelving array with his weapon. His Telxon. He would look at the screen, reading an abbreviated description, *RaguSpagChes*—Meaning *Ragu Spaghetti Sauce Cheese Flavored*. Numerical coordinates on the screen pinpointed a three foot by three-foot shelving area within the entire warehouse as the location of the item—the pick location.

With the clock always ticking, intense visual focus was needed to spot the item jammed into the shelves among competing products. A quick Telxon zap of the found-item's barcode indicated if it was the correct pick. If so, it disappeared off the nightly pick list. Malachi would grab it and place it on a rocket cart.

Because the shelving units are eight-foot tall, much of the work was completed using a ladder. Or for merchandise on skids located on the top shelf, a walk-behind motorized lift was used to raise and lower the freight.

Malachi embraced the physical challenge. And because of the usually intense pace, he would always say, "The time flies."

"When are you taking a break, Dotty?" Malachi said. "It's already a little past twelve."

"Let me finish Infants," Dotty said. "Then I'm ready."

Malachi decided to wait for her, thinking to himself, "Maybe she's the one?"

Even while he was working and almost as soon as he had awoken, as well as when he was getting ready for work, the verse from James, "The fervent prayers of a righteous man are powerful and effective," kept quickening his spirit.

So, he had repeatedly prayed, "God bring one new person to Jesus at Walmart the next meeting. Please God. Please!" And he didn't mean Elysia—she already said she was coming.

During the last three meetings, it was down to Carl, JC, and Martin. After those meetings, Malachi would think to himself, "God, what is going on?"

But now, his vigor was renewed. He was feeling like a, "Burning and a shining light—for Jesus."

"God, one more person."

"God, a new person."

"God, hear my prayer."

And then he heard Dotty, "Infants is complete."

"You're really a good worker, Dotty."

"Work heartily, as to the Lord," Dotty said.

"You're a Believer?" Malachi said.

"I'm part of the remnant," she said.

"Remnant...ah...yeah," Malachi said. "We have...I mean...I'm leading a group here at work, called Jesus at Walmart. We study the Bible and encourage each other in the Lord. Would you want to join us for some Godly fellowship?"

"So what night, what day is this meeting you call Jesus at Walmart...Malachi?" Dotty said with an intense stare as her chin raised up a notch.

"O.K.," Malachi said. "I'm thinking you want exact details here."

"Truth is important to me."

"It's tomorrow night—Thursday. It's at 3:00 A.M. So that means it's on Friday morning—very early."

"Is that the Lord's Day?" Dotty said.

"Well...ah," Malachi said. "Isn't every day the Lord's day?"

"But what day did He specifically command us to make holy? What day should we keep holy, Malachi?"

"I don't think you want me to say that God wants every day holy," Malachi said. "So ah...I'm thinking also...Sunday is not the answer you're looking...ah..."

"Tuesday," Dotty said.

"Tuesday?"

"Exactly. That is what God has ordained in the Ancient Scripture," Dotty said. "Let me explain it to you."

"No, that's O.K.," Malachi said. "I'm going to go get a Coke."

She frowned at Malachi. "A Coke?"

"Well...no I guess..." Malachi said. "O.K. what were you saying?"

"In the Ancient Scriptures, there are cryptic messages. My church has discerned the heart of God regarding the *true* holy day."

Leap

Malachi leaned against the warehouse desk. Dotty sat down on the stool. And like a hunter with a target in the cross hairs, she beaded in on Malachi as he prayed to himself, "God, one more person."

"In Joel 2:5 it declares, 'Like the noise of chariots on the tops of mountains shall they leap, like the noise of a flame of fire that devoureth the stubble, as a strong people set in battle array,'" Dotty said. "And by intensely studying the cryptic message in this scripture, *my church's founders, we call them Elder Guides,* have discovered a clear message from God regarding the Holy Day."

She smiled at Malachi—kind of, "Malachi, it's actually simple to see. I think your heart will burn within you."

Malachi tried not to smile, when in his brain he could hear Martin saying, "Does it cause heartburn?"

"This is serious, Malachi," Dotty said. "*Mountain tops* refers to: the *top* of each year. *Leap* prophetically points to the discovery of Leap Year. So, every time the first day of a Leap Year falls on the Holy Day—and it only happens a few times a century—so it's big news—it's *noise.* So, *a flame of fire that devoureth* means the existing Holy Day is burned up. The *stubble* and dryness of routine is burned away as we change— *Leap* the Holy Day to the next day. And *leap* to a higher place with God. So, when this occurs the next time, the Holy Day will then be on Wednesday. And the *Strong People*, us the remnant, will be *set in battle array.*"

Malachi maintained a monotone facial expression, but in his mind, his index finger was pointing into his wide-open mouth and his head pitched toward the ground.

As Dotty talked on, it seemed without taking a breath, Malachi was looking for an opening to leap into the conversation without shining an LED flashlight into her eyes.

Malachi glanced at his watch when Dotty concluded with, "Does this make sense to you, Malachi? I hope it does, because the Bible says even the very elect shall be deceived."

"Hey, break's almost over," Malachi said. "You're not the one…I mean…you're not interested in coming to Jesus at Walmart?"

She looked at Malachi for a couple of seconds. Her gaze softened. She tenderly touched Malachi's hand, which was gripping the workspace counter, and quickly retracted it, "We need to pray before we go back to work."

"Pray?"

She grinned at Malachi. "You go first."

"Ah…O.K.," Malachi said. "Ah…well… I pray that all followers of Jesus Christ may be one, dear Father. May we all be connected with You, Father God, just as You and Jesus are connected. Father God, may we believers be one, so that the world will believe by this witness that Jesus is the only way. Please send an extra measure of the Holy Spirit so we will know You better and will know our brothers and sisters in the Lord better. Help us to complete the work You have for us here on Earth—as one. Amen."

And then Dotty said, "I pray that the eyes of Malachi's heart may be enlightened, so that he will know what is the hope of Your calling, what are the riches of the glory of Your inheritance to those who follow *all* of Your commandments, especially the one revealed to him tonight—so clearly. And show him what is the surpassing greatness of Your power toward true believers—toward Your remnant, dear God. Amen."

Dotty then said to Malachi, like a mother giving final instructions before her five-year old boarded a school bus, "Malachi, please be willing to pay the cost to search out the truth of religion."

She smiled and pointed her finger heavenward.

"Religion means a lot to you," Malachi said. "Doesn't it, Dotty?"

She nodded her head, "Everything."

30. Mega Millions

It was a late lunch.

Dotty and Malachi had been nearly running to beat the 3:00 A.M. pick-list cutoff time. With minutes to go, they had zapped and carted the last of the items to be wheeled out to the stocking floor.

As he fed the vending machine and punched *Coke*, Malachi heard someone sitting at a table adjacent to the machine say, "Did you hear Mega Millions might go over three-hundred million this week?"

Malachi almost didn't hear the associate because his mind was devising a plan to thwart another round with Dotty tonight. He liked working with her but, "Two rounds in one night," he thought to himself. "I need to get re-fortified."

He didn't see Dotty around, and the break room was

sparse with people.

Malachi turned around with his Coke in his right hand. "No. No I didn't," Malachi said. "That's a ton of money."

"If it goes to three-hundred million, the cash payout would be one-hundred and ninety-three million. Or you could take the annuity. That would be a little over twelve million dollars a year for twenty-six years. That's before taxes. Taxes will run around thirty-four percent. The last time the Mega Millions went over three-hundred million, it was in November of 2005. A group of seven people from Sacramento, California won it. That jackpot went to three-hundred and fifteen million. They say this one probably won't go that high. You never know though; in October of 2009…"

"I'm thinking you like playing the lottery?" Malachi said.

By now, Malachi had made his way around the table and was sitting opposite of the associate. Her eyes and voice had followed him as he found a seat.

Malachi extended his hand. "My name's Malachi. I've never actually introduced myself."

"My name's Vony. Glad to meet you, Malachi."

"You're a cashier; you work the front end," Malachi said. "You started…ah… mid-December?"

"The first week of December."

"So, you're into the lottery and all that."

Vony smiled. Her face brightened. "That and the casino."

Malachi knew the *casino* meant the Little River Casino five miles north of town, owned by the Ojibwa Indian Tribe, a big draw for tourists and the locals.

Vony then glanced to her right and then to her left. She leaned toward Malachi and said in a quieter tone, "They won't let me in the casino. I got arrested for disturbing the peace. I got drunk…and the tribal police—they're every-where up there."

Malachi noticed her countenance and demeanor had shifted. Her shoulders slumped. Her face dimmed.

Vony couldn't hear Malachi.

It was an in-the-brain type prayer.

"God, one more person."

"God, one new person to attend Jesus at Walmart."

"Tomorrow night, God. Hear my prayer."

"Please God."

"Jesus answered my prayer," Vony said.

With her abrupt shift of gears, Malachi didn't stop to ponder what to say. It just popped out, "Do you know Jesus?"

"I pray to Jesus all the time," Vony said. "I prayed, 'Jesus don't let me go to the casino.' I was spending too much money up there. Losing a lot. Then I got arrested. And now they won't let me in the casino."

"Hey, it sounds like you might want to come to Jesus at Walmart tomorrow," Malachi said. And then he went on to explain to her what Jesus at Walmart was all about.

"It's kind of like church?" Vony said.

"Yeah," Malachi said. "Kind of like that. But small. And really good people attend. What do you think?"

"I've just never got into church," Vony said. "But I do watch six or seven hours of Christian television every week. That's my church."

"I'm not against that," Malachi said. "But the Bible tells us to gather together. People meeting together as God's family is important to God."

With her right hand, Vony touched the area of her heart. "I think church is what you make it in here."

She looked intently at Malachi. "It's about the heart. What a person feels in their heart."

"Do you know what the Bible says about the human heart, Vony? It says…"

"No, I don't," Vony said before Malachi could continue.

"But I do know Jesus answered my prayer. And I didn't have to go to church for that to happen or any Bible study group."

"And it's just easier that way," Malachi said. "Right?"

"Yeah…easier," Vony said. "And that's how I like it."

Malachi turned his head to the right. He stared at the wall for a few moments. And then said in a nearly-silent whisper, "No cost."

"What did you say, Malachi?"

31. ee

"Malachi, what's that?" Sal said. She pointed with her right hand, which was holding a Telxon.

Sitting off to the side of the walkway leading to the backroom, on a skid, sat a floor display.

They would arrive from a variety of vendors about once a week. The skid would be pulled to the floor, the cardboard removed to reveal the product. A Walmart— SAVE MONEY, LIVE BETTER, plopped on top—with the pricing—UNBEAT-ABLE. And then…let the shopping begin.

"I didn't really…notice…pay any attention to it," Malachi said. "It's been a little wild back here tonight."

"Didn't notice it," Sal said as she glanced at her watch. "Shift's over in twenty-four minutes." She flicked the Telxon toward the display, scanning its barcode. "This needs to be out on the floor— now. Right now!"

Malachi scurried to find a pallet jack and hollered to Dotty, who was zapping and hurling incoming overstock onto the metal shelves. "I've got to run this display out to the floor."

Dotty threw a glance his way and said, "O.K." as she snatched another loaded rocket cart.

As Malachi plowed the pallet jack under the skid, Sal said, "This needs to be set in the southeast corner of action alley. I'll meet you there in three minutes."

Off she sped.

Malachi spun around and, with the pallet jack handles behind him, like a horse pulling a plow, he raced out of the warehouse.

Less than a minute after he lowered the skid at its designated location, he saw Sal charging toward him. She was holding her walkie-talkie, pressed against her face as her left hand flailed in the air above her head.

As Malachi watched her, his mind traveled back to a conversation they had had not long after he started working at Walmart.

When she said it, her candor had surprised him. "If I wasn't hard-nosed, everybody would walk all over me."

Malachi had thought, "She's right."

"I'm graded on a scorecard every night, on every aspect of what we get accomplished, and how well it's done. Every night."

Her tone softened. Malachi wondered why she was confiding in him, "It's really harsh sometimes. The pressure is almost more...I ah...really need this job. I just don't know where to turn sometimes."

And then Malachi refocused on Sal striding toward him. He fervently—and quickly—prayed.

"God, one more person."

"God, one more person at Jesus at Walmart."

"God, hear my prayer."

"What are you waiting for?" Sal barked as she stopped right in front of Malachi. "Get the cardboard off of it. Now."

Malachi whipped out his box cutter, and in less than a minute he had the cardboard stripped off of the display, which was the size of two filing cabinets set back to back.

"That's what I need," he heard Sal say as he finished flattening the cardboard and placing it on the pallet jack. "Eternal Energy."

Blazoned across the black display in bold, blood-red letters were the words: ETERNAL ENERGY SHOTS. Below, cardboard trays were tilted at a twenty-degree angle to display hundreds of bottles of elixir. Each one was the size of a whiteout container. Inside was a concoction of twenty-five vitamins, amino acids, antioxidants, and more. In various flavors—berry, grape, tropical punch, and pomegranate.

Below the four tiers of shelves and an interlocked *ee* logo were the words: *making your life better.* The vibrant green letters looked almost handwritten, like a note from a friend.

"Done," Malachi said.

And when he looked up, he could see a glimmer of moistness in Sal's eyes.

In front of the now-ready Walmart display, they stood motionless. Malachi felt the beat of his heart.

"I told myself that this year I was going to quit being that way," Sal said. "I'm sorry, Malachi."

To Malachi, it felt like a mother pulling back the curtain of her soul to her child.

"Why would I treat you this way?" Sal said. "I'm under pressure…and I'm…you're such a good worker. Such a good man."

"It's O.K.," Malachi said. "I under…"

"No, it's not," she said as she shook her head. "And it's affecting my health."

Sal's gaze fell toward the floor. Malachi shifted his eyes to the right—looking at the display. Neither one said anything for a couple of seconds.

And then Malachi said, "Well...we have some Eternal Energy Shots right here, Sal. Guaranteed to fix everything in your life. Instantly."

Sal raised her head and looked over at the display and then at Malachi and said, "Making your life better."

They both smiled.

"Making your life better," Malachi said slowly. "Have you ever noticed that even good products, healthy products need to be advertised a bunch. Over and over and over again. If something is so good for a person…"

He tapped the top of the *ee* display with his right hand. "I'm not sure about this stuff…maybe. But something that's really good for a person—even if they know it, it has to be brought to their attention repeatedly. Why do you think that is?"

Sal grinned. "I know where you're heading."

"Can't sneak it up on you," Malachi said. "So, can I just give you the Walmart-style making-your-life-better full-page advertisement?"

"As a penitence for my behavior?"

As if on its own accord, Malachi's right hand softly touched Sal's left shoulder. "I care about you, Sal. It matters to me what happens in your life." And then his hand retreated.

"I know you do. I know you do, Malachi."

"Here's my advertisement," Malachi said. "Jesus at Walmart is tomorrow. You know the time. You know the place. Sal, I saw God touch you—at Stu's funeral. And the time you attended Jesus at Walmart. Maybe you need another touch. Or how about this? Maybe a big hug from God. Maybe something ongoing…not just a sip."

"Maybe," Sal said.

Malachi scrunched his face a little and then said, "You're willing to pay the cost for a career you think you want. But now you're not sure about that. The cost is turning out to be more than…ah… I guess maybe, more than you expected."

"Yeah…I ah…yeah."

"You have this battle going on," Malachi said as he stretched out his hands with the palms up. "You're weighing things out like on a balance scale. On the left, the cost of your career. On the right, the cost of seeking Jesus…of following Jesus."

Malachi rocked his hands back and forth. "Choose this day. Who will you serve, Sal?"

"I never thought of it that way," Sal said. "You know what? I need to come to your meeting."

32. God...One More Person

The chairs for the weekly Jesus at Walmart meeting were set up in the corner to the right of the door. In a room that could hold a couple hundred people, Malachi had placed eight chairs in a semi-circle facing away from the door.

Malachi's seat faced the semi-circle with a view to the door—the door leading to the store's foyer. Resting on a stand behind his chair was his mandolin—the one Martin had given him two days ago.

In addition, he had a table immediately inside the door with Bibles and a handout for the night's meeting and the left-over Jesus at Walmart flyers. It was arranged self-serve style with notes: *Please Take One.*

He sat in his chair—

Praying:

"God, one more person."

"God, one more person tonight."

"Please God. Hear my prayer."

At 2:55, he noticed movement near the door. It was Carl. And Elysia was with him.

Malachi smiled when he saw Carl.

And smiled even more when he said to Elysia, "Thank you so much for coming tonight. It's kind of late for most people."

"I would stay up all night to see God do something special," Elysia said.

"Yeah...Yeah," Malachi said.

As they were talking, JC arrived from home. And Martin, who had been stocking in the Hardware Department, arrived just after she greeted Malachi.

At 3:03, Malachi said, "Hey, why don't we sit down. Grab one of tonight's handouts. Let's get started."

After everyone had found a seat, he looked over at the door once more.

"Welcome to Jesus at Walmart," Malachi said. He blinked his eyes as the faces of Dotty, Vony, and Sal flashed into his mind.

And then he heard Martin say, "I talked to some people about coming down here tonight. I don't know though."

"Me too," Malachi said. "I kept praying the last two days that God would send one more person tonight." He smiled and looked at Elysia. "Besides you. I knew you were coming."

Malachi glanced at his watch—3:05, and then the door. Then he said to Martin, "Could you pray to launch us into what God has for us tonight?"

"Dear God, give us childlike faith," Martin said. "You've heard our prayers. We don't know Your plan or..."

"Malachi," a voice called out.

Everyone looked up.

It was Alex.

Malachi rushed over to him. "What's wrong Alex? What's wrong!"

Alex smiled and hugged Malachi. "Nothing. Really. Nothing's wrong."

"Alex, what are you doing here?" Malachi said. "Does your mom know you're here?"

"She's never home," Alex said. "I'm always home by myself at night."

"Your grandma doesn't watch you like she used to?"

"Mom's mad at her. They don't talk anymore."

"Why didn't you ever tell me this when we were together?"

Alex shifted his eyes toward the floor.

"Alex, look at me," Malachi said. "It's O.K. I just want to know why you didn't tell me before."

"If Mom found out I told you...she...she wouldn't let me see you anymore."

Malachi rubbed Alex's shoulder. "So what made you come down to Walmart in the middle of the night?"

"Mom used to come to this meeting. I remember," Alex said. "I woke up tonight...for some reason. Remember when I heard the voice in my head that said we should give Elysia a gift?"

"Yeah," Malachi smiled, "I sure do Alex."

"This time...well it's hard to explain," Alex said. "But... well...I...can I stay?"

"This is a serious adult Bible study," Malachi said. "Everyone here is a..."

"You can stay, Alex," Carl said.

Malachi turned around and looked Carl directly in the eye. Carl nodded.

"Well...yeah," Malachi said. "Grab a Bible and a seat, Alex."

"Praise God," Martin said as he power punched the air. "Thank you, God. One more person—praise God."

Alex grinned.

As everyone sat down again, Malachi reached behind his chair and wrapped the fingers of his left hand around the neck of the mandolin and flipped the leather strap over his body. He sat down. His eyes briefly fell on each person—Carl, Martin, JC, Elysia, Alex.

He heard a voice in his head, "Delight yourself in the Lord and He will give you the desires of your heart."

He nodded his head and then heard more, "Malachi, make sure you know the desire of your heart is the right desire."

With the mandolin hanging from his neck, Malachi held his Bible in his hands and leaned forward as he read:

Wake up soul! Wake up harp! Wake up lute! Wake up you sleepyhead sun!

I'm thanking You, God, out loud in the streets, singing Your praises in town and country. The deeper Your love, the higher it goes; every cloud is a flag to Your faithfulness. Soar high in the skies, O God! Cover the whole earth with Your glory!

Malachi took a deep breath. And exhaled, "Wow."

He glanced at the floor and then raised his eyes. And strummed his mandolin, "Is it O.K. to feel the awesomeness of God...so much that..."

His eyes fell back to the floor.

It was more than a few seconds before Malachi looked up. He breathed in slowly before he said, "Praise the Lord with me—with this song He gave me."

> Awesome is the God
> Awesome is the God
> Awesome is the God, Most High
>
> Worthy
> Worthy

God...One More Person

Worthy

Worthy is the Lord
Worthy is the Lord
Worthy is the Lord, who died upon a cross

Here's my life
Have your way

For You Lord
For You Lord
No cost is too great

Awesome is the God
Awesome is the God
Awesome is the God, Most High

Alex's exuberance far outpaced everyone else's. He sang out, "Awesome is the God," as his body swayed in his seat.

When Malachi finished, Alex said, "Let's sing some more."

"Maybe next week," Malachi said. "Remember I told you that this is a serious adult Bible study. You still want to stay?"

"Yeah."

"Since JC and Martin are going to be baptized in two weeks, I thought we should talk about what the Bible says about baptism," Malachi said. "And we know that baptism is a way for a person to show others that they are a follower of Jesus Christ."

Malachi began to explain the basics of baptism, but then he saw Alex waving his hand back and forth.

"Alex, do you have a question?"

"Does it cost anything?"

"Are you asking if JC and Martin have to pay to be baptized?"

"Yeah."

"No, there's no cost," Malachi said.

"But...I mean everything costs here at Walmart...even free food—somebody has to pay for it. For them to be baptized, it must have cost somebody something," Alex said. "Who paid the cost?"

Author's Note

Dear Reader,

During the writing of **Jesus at Walmart...the Cost**, a red curtain was drawn diagonally across a room. Splitting the room in half. This former bedroom was my writing den.

So, I become closed off from the world. There were many hours of solitude behind the red curtain.

Many, many nights. Many, many days.

Solitude—me and the words. But I'm not alone, I would always have a sense that God was near. The writing journey is a spiritual journey for me. Way more than I could ever fully convey with words.

My hope/prayer is that your reading of **Jesus at Walmart... the Cost** will be a time when you will grow closer to God. It will be spiritual journey.

Dear Reader: "Thank you for being a part of the **Jesus at Walmart** adventure!" The final book in the Trilogy completes the adventure. It is entitled, **Jesus at Walmart...fire on the Earth**.

It's always a great pleasure to hear from you. You can email me at **rickleland1@outlook.com**. And if you've enjoyed the book, please share a review on **Amazon**. It really helps others discover my works. Thank you so much! And please visit: **rickleland.com** for more books and info.

Before I sign off, I want to send out my gratitude.

Thank You, Father God, without you there would be no **Jesus at Walmart**. I would not be a writer.

To you my dear wife, Nancy, thank you. Without you, there would be no **Jesus at Walmart**. I would not be a writer.

...Rick Leland

Addendum-The Bible Verses

Listed below are the Bible verses found in **Jesus at Walmart...the Cost**. Included is the full Scripture and it's reference.

Dedication

Psalm 110:3   "Your people will volunteer freely in the day of Your power."

Chapter 3

1 Corinthians 1:27   "But God hath chosen the foolish things of the world to confound the wise; and God hath chosen the weak things of the world to confound the things which are mighty."

Isaiah 6:8   "Then I heard the voice of the Lord saying, 'Whom shall I send And who will go for us?' And I said, 'Here am I. Send me!'"

Psalm 37:4   "Delight yourself in the Lord and He will give you the desires of your heart." (Also found in Chapter 4, 7, and 32.)

Chapter 4

Psalm 37:5   "Commit your way to the Lord, trust also in Him, and He will do it." (Also found in Chapter 7)

Chapter 5

2 Corinthians 4:7-17   "We have this treasure in earthen vessels, so that the surpassing greatness of the power will be of God and not from ourselves. We are afflicted in every way, but not crushed. Perplexed, but not despairing. Persecuted,

but not forsaken. Struck down, but not destroyed. Always carrying about in the body, the dying of Jesus. So that the life of Jesus also may be manifested in our body.

For we who live are constantly being delivered over to death for Jesus' sake, so that the life of Jesus also may be manifested in our mortal flesh. So death works in us, but life in you.

But having the same spirit of faith, according to what is written, 'I believe, therefore I spoke,' we also believe, therefore we also speak, knowing that He who raised the Lord Jesus will raise us also with Jesus and will present us with you.

For all things are for your sake, so that the grace which is spreading to more and more people may cause the giving of thanks to abound to the glory of God.

Therefore we do not lose heart, but though our outer man is decaying, yet our inner man is being renewed day by day. For momentary, light affliction is producing for us an eternal weight of glory far beyond all comparison."

Chapter 6

2 Corinthians 4:16-17   "Therefore we do not lose heart, but though our outer man is decaying, yet our inner man is being renewed day by day. For momentary, light affliction is producing for us an eternal weight of glory far beyond all comparison."

John 16:33   "These things I have spoken to you, that in Me you may have peace. In the world you will have tribulation; but be of good cheer, I have overcome the world."

Chapter 7

Psalm 42:5-11   "Why are you in despair, O my soul? And why have you become disturbed within me? Hope in God, for I shall again praise Him for the help of His presence.

O my God, my soul is in despair within me; Therefore I remember You from the land of the Jordan and the peaks of Hermon, from Mount Mizar.

Deep calls to deep at the sound of Your waterfalls; all Your breakers and Your waves have rolled over me.

The LORD will command His lovingkindness in the daytime; and His song will be with me in the night. A prayer to the God of my life. I will say to God my rock, 'Why have You forgotten me? Why do I go mourning because of the oppression of the enemy?'

As a shattering of my bones, my adversaries revile me. While they say to me all day long, 'Where is your God?' Why are you in despair, O my soul? And why have you become disturbed within me? Hope in God, for I shall yet praise Him, the help of my countenance and my God."

Chapter 8

John 10:10 "The thief does not come except to steal, and to kill, and to destroy. I have come that they may have life, and that they may have it more abundantly." (Also found in Chapter 17.)

John 10:11 "I am the good shepherd. The good shepherd gives His life for the sheep."

Chapter 9

Proverbs 5:3 "For the lips of an adulterous woman drip honey and smoother than oil is her speech. But in the end she is bitter as wormwood. Sharp as a two-edged sword."

Chapter 10

Psalms 37:23 "The steps of a good man are established

by the Lord and He delights in his way. When he falls, he will not be hurled headlong, because the Lord is the One who holds him with His hand."

Chapter 11

2 Corinthians 3:18 "But we all, with unveiled face, beholding as in a mirror the glory of the Lord, are being transformed into the same image from glory to glory, just as from the Lord, the Spirit."

Chapter 12

2 Corinthians 4:17 "For momentary, light affliction is producing for us an eternal weight of glory far beyond all comparison."

Lamintations 3:22-23 "The steadfast love of the Lord never ceases; His mercies never come to an end; they are new every morning; great is Your faithfulness."

Chapter 13

Psalm 44:13-19 "Thou makest us a reproach to our neighbours, a scorn and a derision to them that are round about us.

Thou makest us a byword among the heathen, a shaking of the head among the people. My confusion is continually before me, and the shame of my face hath covered me. For the voice of him that reproacheth and blasphemeth; by reason of the enemy and avenger. All this is come upon us; yet have we not forgotten Thee, neither have we dealt falsely in Thy covenant.

Our heart is not turned back, neither have our steps declined from Thy way; though thou hast sore broken us in the place of dragons (jackals), and covered us with the shadow of death. "

Ecclesiastes 7:1 "A good name is better than precious

ointment; and the day of death than the day of one's birth."

Numbers 32:23   "But if ye will not do so, behold, ye have sinned against the Lord: and be sure your sin will find you out."

Chapter 14

1 Corithians 2:2   "For I determined not to know anything among you, save Jesus Christ, and Him crucified."

Chapter 15

Psalm 19:14   "Let the words of my mouth and the meditation of my heart be acceptable in Your sight, O Lord—my Strength and my Redeemer."

Chapter 16

Jeremiah 29:11   "For I know the plans I have for you, declares the Lord. Plans to prosper you and not harm you. Plans to give you hope and a future."

Hebrews 12:2   "Let us fix our eyes on Jesus, the author and finisher of our faith. Who for the joy set before Him endured the cross, scorning its shame, and sat down at the right hand of the throne of God."

Romans 3:23   "For all have sinned and fallen short of the glory of God."

Chapter 17

Psalm 24:3-4   "Who may ascend into the hill of the Lord? And who may stand in His holy place? He who has clean hands and a pure heart, who does not lift up his soul to an idol or swear by what is false."

1 Corinthians 2:3-5   "I was with you in weakness and in fear and in much trembling. And my message and my preaching were not in persuasive words of wisdom. But in demonstration of the Spirit and of power, so that your faith would not rest on the wisdom of men, but on the power of God."

Chapter 18

Psalm 86:4   "Make glad the soul of Your servant. For to You, O Lord, I lift up my soul."

2 Timothy 4:3-5   "The time will come when people will not listen to sound doctrine, but will follow their own desires and will collect for themselves more and more teachers who will tell them what they are itching to hear.
    They will turn away from listening to the truth and give their attention to legends.
    But you must keep control of yourself in all circumstances. Endure suffering, do the work of a preacher of the Good News and perform your whole duty as a servant of God."

Chapter 22

Psalm 34:18-20   "The Lord is near to the brokenhearted. And saves those who are crushed in spirit. Many are the afflictions of the righteous; but the Lord delivers him out of them all. He keeps all his bones. Not one of them is broken."

Chapter 23

Matthew 5:8   "Blessed are the pure in heart, for they shall see God."

Romans 1:17   "For therein is the righteousness of God revealed from faith to faith: as it is written, The just shall live by faith."

Chapter 24

Galatians 2:20   "I have been crucified with Christ and it is no longer I who live, but Christ lives in me. And the life which I now live in the flesh I live by faith in the Son of God, who loved me and gave Himself up for me."

Leviticus 23:27   "On exactly the tenth day of this seventh month is the day of atonement; it shall be a holy convocation for you, and you shall humble your souls and present an offering by fire to the LORD." (Also found in Chapter 27.)

Luke 24:32   "Were not our hearts burning within us while He was speaking to us on the road, while He was explaining the Scriptures to us?"

Chapter 25

Acts 11:24   "Barnabas was a good man, full of the Holy Spirit and faith, and a great number were brought to the Lord."

Acts 11:25   "Then Barnabas went to Tarsus to look for Paul."

Acts 2:2   "And suddenly there came from heaven a noise like a violent rushing wind, and it filled the whole house where they were sitting."

Chapter 26

Psalm 40:1:17   "I waited patiently for the Lord's help. Then He listened to me and heard my cry. He pulled me out of a dangerous pit—out of the deadly quicksand. He set me safely on a rock and made me secure.

He taught me to sing a new song. A song of praise to our God. Many who see this will take warning and will put their trust in the Lord.

Blessed are those who trust the Lord, who do not turn to idols or join those who worship false gods.

You have done many things for us, O Lord our God. There is no one like You! You have made many wonderful plans for us. I could never speak of them all—their number is so great!

You do not want sacrifices and offerings. You do not ask for animals burned whole on the altar or for sacrifices to take away sins. Instead, You have given me ears to hear You and so I answered, 'Here I am;' Your instructions for me are in the Book of the Law. How I love to do Your will, my God! I keep Your teaching in my heart.

In the assembly of all your people, Lord, I told the Good News that You save us. You know that I will never stop telling it. I have not kept the news of salvation to myself. I have always spoken of Your faithfulness and help. In the assembly of all Your people I have not been silent about Your loyalty and constant love.

I know You will never stop being merciful to me. Your love and loyalty will always keep me safe.

I am surrounded by many troubles—too many to count! My sins have caught up with me and I can no longer see. They are more than the hairs of my head and I have lost my courage.

Save me, Lord! Help me now!

May those who try to kill me be completely defeated and confused. May those who are happy because of my troubles be turned back and disgraced. May those who make fun of me be dismayed by their defeat.

May all who come to You be glad and joyful. May all who are thankful for Your salvation always say, 'How great is the Lord!'

I am weak and poor, O Lord, but You have not forgotten me. You are my Savior and my God. Do not delay, O my God."

Hebrews 4:12   "For the Word of God is living and active and sharper than any two-edged sword."

Chapter 27

Matthew 10:37-39   "Anyone who loves his father or mother more than Me is not worthy of Me. Anyone who loves his son or daughter more than Me is not worthy of Me. And anyone who does not take up his cross and follow Me is not worthy of Me. Whoever finds his life will lose it and whoever loses his life for My sake will find it."

Deuteronomy 19:15   "One witness shall not rise against a man concerning any iniquity or any sin that he commits; by the mouth of two or three witnesses the matter shall be established."

Ecclesiastes 4:12   "Two people can resist an attack that would defeat one person alone. A rope made of three cords is hard to break."

Zechariah 4:6   "It's not by power, it's not by might, but by My Spirit says the Lord."

Chapter 28

Acts 4:32   "The group of believers was one in mind and heart. None of them said that any of their belongings were their own, but they all shared with one another everything they had."

Galatians 6:7   "Do not be deceived, God is not mocked; for whatever a man sows, that shall he also reap."

1 Corinthians 1:27   "But God has chosen the foolish things of the world to confound the wise; and God has chosen the weak things of the world to confound the things which are mighty."

Chapter 29

John 5:35   "He (John) was a burning and a shining light: and you were willing for a season to rejoice in his light."

Colossians 3:23   "And whatsoever ye do, do it heartily, as to the Lord, and not unto men."

Matthew 24:24   "For there shall arise false Christs and false prophets, and shall show great signs and wonders; insomuch that, if it were possible, they shall deceive the very elect."

Chapter 32

Psalm 57:8-11   "Wake up soul! Wake up harp! Wake up lute! Wake up you sleepyhead sun! I'm thanking You, God, out loud in the streets, singing Your praises in town and country.
The deeper Your love, the higher it goes; every cloud is a flag to Your faithfulness. Soar high in the skies, O God! Cover the whole earth with Your glory!"

Made in United States
Orlando, FL
27 December 2024

56607937R00131